Twins of Prey

W.C. Hoffman

Want to stay up to date with W.C. Hoffman and the **Twins of Prey** series?

Join his mailing list and become a "**Twin**."

https://wchoffman.weebly.com/

All "**Twins**" receive a free short story and discounted prices on future

books.

ACKNOWLEDGMENTS

This work would not have been possible without the lifelong hunting, fishing, and overall life guidance I have received from my Uncle Tom. For an amount of time in my life, I had no father figure, and Tom was there for me. Tom is my biological father's cousin with two sons of his own who never left me behind. To my cousins, Cory and Cody, thank you for sharing your dad with me when I needed him the most.

Throughout these stories you will read Uncle's voice. When I wrote them, I could hear Tom's voice. Tom was a wonderful storyteller, musician, teacher, and prankster. Uncle teaches the boys many things that Tom also taught me. Rest assured not all of Uncle's teachings are derived from my own lessons, but many were.

My "Uncle" left us unexpectedly, on his own accord, in early December 2012. I hope he knows I have come to understand and forgive him. It is not what he took away from us, it is what he left behind that means the most.

Rest well beside the birch trees, Uncle Tom. We miss you every day.

1 LIFE

They knew this day would come. It had to. After all, they knew all too well that all things live and all things die. It was one of the many life lessons Uncle had taught them, and Uncle himself was no different. They knew one day Uncle would be dead, and they would be alone. Uncle had decided that today, December 4th, was that day.

Thirteen years ago, on a remote northern Michigan two-lane stretch of dirt road that passed through miles of national forest, the man the twins would come to know as Uncle found an overturned truck while hunting turkeys with his bow in a hard, pouring rain. Stalking slowly up to the red, rusted mid-1970s 4x4, he recognized the unforgettable smell. Death was in the area. Slumped over the torn leather seats, with yellow cushioning escaping from the missing seams, was a woman driver. Bleeding heavily, hardly breathing and barely alive, she could not easily speak, but what she did say was clear.

"Take."

Uncle had a hard time hearing her over the static coming from the AM radio coupled with the unforgiving rain pounding on the roof and windshield. However, he could see her eyes were full of passion and fear as she peered at Uncle through the broken glass of the passenger window. Uncle felt her eyes on his soul, and he could not look away.

Uncle forced open the damaged passenger door to find two car seats.

"Take … the …," she gasped while bleeding from a large gash that ran along her neck to the middle of her armpit.

The three-year-old boys looked at Uncle. They didn't cry or scream, just looked. Their dark black faces gave way to the brightness of the whiteness in their eyes. They seemed to have the same grasping eye quality that belonged to their dying mother.

"Take … them," again she labored.

Uncle reached in, wiped the blood from her eyes and assured her, "They will be safe."

This is not the version of the story that the twins know. Uncle told and taught them everything they do know, but the truth about their mother was never explained to them.

Tomek and Drake do know that they were found in a truck, alone. However, Uncle took the truth about their mother to his grave.

He figured there would come a time when they would need to know, yet he was never able to bring himself to talk about it. It was not that he felt guilty. Uncle knew he did what he had to do. He just did not think the truth would help the boys survive, which was his ultimate goal.

The twins and Uncle had talked about his death quite regularly in the past few years. Uncle was a large man with failing knees who suffered from a string of constant migraine headaches. Uncle had made many more trips to town than normal in the last few years to obtain medication for his unforgiving migraines.

The boys secretly blamed each trip for his worsening conditions, further instilling their desire to never leave their home in the woods. It was planned that his body was to be burned alongside the river and his ashes spread in the wood line to the east of their cabin. There was a clump of birch trees that Uncle had grown fond of as a hunting spot. Both boys had killed their first deer in that stretch of birch. This would be Uncle's final resting place.

And so it was done on that cold, wet, raining day in December. Uncle walked out to the river and took his own life. Uncle was gone.

Luckily enough, the winter gave way quickly to a beautiful spring. Not every spring is like this in northern Michigan. The woods they called home had everything they needed to survive. Being more than thirty miles deep from any road or sign of civilization, it was an oasis where hunting and fishing opportunities were endless. The twins knew of the outside world from the crossing air traffic, but only Drake had been there.

Uncle took him into the smallest town near them one winter at age seven for a bad case of pneumonia. Drake was hospitalized as an orphan and recovered quickly. He soon realized he was a source of activity in the hospital. Cars and vans with towers on the top began to arrive on the second day of his stay. On the third night, a nurse snuck into his room and woke him up. It was the first time he had seen another person with dark skin besides himself and his brother. She asked him many questions regarding who he was and where he lived. Drake had been trained for this by Uncle and only answered with the information that Uncle had presented to him.

"Who is your mother?" she asked.

Drake sat, silent and confused.

"Do you have a twin brother?" she quickly asked next.

Drake knew then that somehow the nurse was aware of Tomek. He looked into her eyes and replied with the words Uncle told him to use in situations like this.

"I do not feel well. I need to lie down."

The nurse reverted to her caregiver nature and eased him back into a sleeping position where he remained awake the rest of the night, pondering his next move.

Hours after sundown, it grew quiet as it did the previous night. This gave Drake a sense of security he knew he could exploit. He looked around the room, waiting on the sick boy placed next to him to fall asleep.

Drake exhaled a sigh of relief as he removed the wires and electrodes hooked to his arm and chest. Drake felt like one of the many rabbits he had caught in his own snare traps. Being free and untangled never felt so good.

Bing, Bing, Bing ...

The monitoring machine sounded, which caused the dark-skinned nurse to quickly return and reattach him. Drake rethought his plan after carefully watching the nurse remove the plugs from the machine's main head piece and push a yellow button on the screen. This seemed to stop the alarm from going off.

As she replaced the wires on him, she scolded, "Everything on that machine comes right to our desk so we can watch you and make sure you are doing okay from there, honey."

"*Honey?*" he thought to himself and rolled his eyes. "*Honey is what we trap bears and bugs with.*"

Drake wondered which one the nurse was, a bear or a bug.

An hour or two had gone by and again Drake waited, awake and knowing that the shift change for the nursing staff came at about five a.m., as far as he could tell from the sunlight creeping through the window. At five a.m. on the dot, Drake got out of bed and wheeled his monitor over to the bedside of his roommate. Quickly removing the plugs from the head of the machine, he pressed the yellow button. He then removed the patches on his body and began to replace them on the unsuspecting boy.

This caused the boy to roll over and wake up. Looking at Drake in his sleepy daze, wondering what he was doing, the boy attempted to yell, *"Nur ..."*

Drake silenced him with an elbow strike straight to the temple, rendering the child immediately unconscious.

"Head, throat, gut." He could hear Uncle's voice preaching to him of the three places that would cause a victim to go silent. Drake quickly rigged the boy with the leads and plugged them back into the monitor.

Beep, Beep ... silence ...

As far as the nurses were concerned, Drake was fast asleep and wouldn't need to be checked on until breakfast rounds in a few hours. Drake removed all the sheets from both beds and the curtains. Tying them together, he draped them out the window anchored to the bed leg inside the room. The window faced east. Drake knew this from watching the sun rise. Drake knew he would be headed west. He figured the distraction would buy him some time, if he needed it.

Then, shortly later at first light, seven-year-old Drake exited his hospital room, calmly walked out the front doors, past the unmanned news and police vehicles, and entered the wood line just west of the parking lot.

The plan was for Drake to meet with Uncle at the big pine, a staggering tree that was the only landmark visible from both the town and their woodland home. It was their meeting place in the event of an emergency. Uncle taught them to go to the pine if they were lost, and that is exactly what Drake did.

Hours later he found Uncle there, waiting for him. Drake hiked all eleven miles into the thick woods in only slippers and a gown. With no food, no water, and no weapons, Drake found the pine and was not surprised to see both Tomek and Uncle there waiting for him.

This scare led Uncle to be more cautious with the twins. It also meant he had to explain more of the world outside of the woods to them. They were soon educated in the basics of reading, writing, arithmetic and, of course, government. The basics were taught the same way as any other child would have learned them. However, their education of government, especially the United States government, was shaded by Uncle's dark past as a high-ranking and ultimately disgraced military instructor. Uncle made sure they knew about the dangers of men and war.

Uncle explained to them that before his life in the woods, he taught thousands of young government men how to kill. As a Gunnery Sergeant in the Marine Corp's survival school, Uncle lived by the teachings of the SERE. Survival, Evasion, Resistance, and Escape were the backbone of each of his graduates. Much like the Marines that Uncle trained, the twins were also taught how to fight, hide, escape, be silent, and how to kill tactically, if needed. By age nine, Uncle felt they were better trained in the way of the woods and of war than any previous man he had sent to die.

Uncle warned them that one day they would be forced to interact with the others, and if they had to, they would need to fight. Compassion and love were a weakness in their world, and if they had to kill, they would have neither of those for their prey.

"You must operate and move in the shadows of the woods. If seen, you will evaporate into the thick," Uncle warned them. "You must kill to survive, or you will not."

For the boys, killing their enemy was no different than killing a deer. Anything that ensures you live to see the next day. Survival is all that mattered; survival was all that was taught.

Uncle had made sure they could survive on their own. Both boys were skilled in all facets of the outdoors. Hunting and fishing with equipment they made by hand. Bows carved from saplings and cedar arrows, which were adorned with turkey-feather fletching and sharpened stone points. Dead fall and pit traps also were regularly used on everything from squirrels and deer to the occasional black bear. There was not an animal in the world they could not track, hunt, bait, trap, kill, clean, and eat.

"If it moves, it's food," Uncle often would say.

Uncle had also taught each boy how to garden and live off the land. Tomatoes, potatoes, beans, squash, and even pumpkins were grown from seed each year. Every crop was preserved for the winter months and fiercely defended against wildlife invaders. An eight-foot wide, eight-foot deep pit trap surrounded the entire three-acre garden, leaving the garden only accessible by foot bridges that had to be lowered by hand. It took the three of them two full springs and summers to dig it. However, it provided them not only with crop security, but many unlucky deer and bears fell into the pit each season. Tomek and Drake quickly learned that prey in a trap is easier to kill than hunting it in the wild.

Once they reached age ten, the duties were split with each boy swapping jobs the next year. One spent the year working the garden and gathering supplies, while the other tended to the traps and hunted.

The following year the roles would be switched. Uncle knew he would soon be leaving this world, and he knew the twins would be okay with the world. What Uncle could never have known was if the world would be okay with the twins.

2 HOME

"The roof needs new moss and thatch," Tomek said, yawning from inside his bunk.

"Have fun with that," Drake replied. "I have about forty traps to check, and we still have that venison hanging, waiting to be butchered."

Tomek grew annoyed with his brother in the years Drake was hunting. It was Tomek's favorite job, and he loved every minute of it.

"You do understand that if we don't get the roof completely mossed over and some more field grass growing on top of us, the entire house will be visible?" Tomek's sarcastic tone was evident but was met with a heavier dose of snark.

"You should probably get out of bed, then, and get to it. You know, the roof is very important, Tomek." Drake smirked while rolling over.

"You think?" Tomek replied, keeping the sarcasm high.

"All the time. You should try it now and then. It won't kill ya," Drake laughed with his head buried into the soft pillow.

The truth was both of them knew the roof was important. Going from three workers to two did make it harder on the boys until they eventually realized exactly how many supplies Uncle required just for himself. Scaling back on their food production, weapons, and other supplies allowed them time to work on the things that mattered. Today it was the roof.

The cabin was a simple one-room design with built-in defenses. It nested into the hillside on three sides, and when the roof was properly camouflaged, the small cabin was virtually invisible to anyone beyond thirty yards away. Even the door was carved from a massive oak that had been struck by lightning several years before. It looked like a solid piece that lay on the ground, but it was hollow and swung open on wooden hinges. Uncle had built it this way. His design relied on the hill for protection in the harsh winter and cooler underground temps in the summer.

Not only was their home adequate protection from the weather and casual flyovers, it was also rigged to be the ideal stronghold. Over the years they had dug a simple tunnel system that led to a room draped in rocks from floor to ceiling. This room happened to be downhill from the main living area and was dug directly under the river. Uncle used this room as both the kitchen and the furnace. A simple stove was crafted from the existing rock edge, and the chimney pipe ran up and into the river. This allowed them to cook inside and heat the cabin undetected.

Uncle had designed the special chimney pipe with a one-way valve on the end. The smoke would be released underwater and never become airborne. The wood stove also did a remarkable job at radiating upwards and heating the rest of the home. The main living area was small but comfortable. Wood-crafted floors with loose limestone gravel near the door would alert them when someone walked in, no matter where they were located within the depths of the tunnel system.

Uncle and the twins had frequently layered the walls and ceilings with birch bark over the years. The white tone of the bark gathered and reflected light from their torch lamps and combined with a natural mineral derived from gypsum called alabaster, which was taken from the river muck. The interior had a fireproof, concrete-like consistency. The naturally formed walls held back the dirt walls of the hill and was strong enough to hang the handmade counters and pantries they had built. Above the door on the inside of the cabin hung a framed Band-Aid.

"No single part of the Band-Aid can do the job alone," Uncle often told the boys. "Three parts must work together, okay?" Uncle lowered his voice. "The two sides can stick together and hold on. However, if they are joined by the middle piece, then not only can they hold on, but they can do it together and heal. Three parts make it strong and give it a reason to hold on."

The boys were not surprised when a Band-Aid reference made it into their life lessons, as "Band-Aid" was Uncle's nickname growing up as a young teen. As it was told to them by Uncle, the nickname had been earned for all the hours he had spent working as a medic on his father's ambulance.

Table, chairs, pantries, cupboards, weapon racks, and beds rounded out the rest of the cabin's charm. It was all they needed. It was home.

The charm, however, was deceiving. What was built to help survive and hide was also built to kill. Multiple passages were dug that led to deep pitfall traps. They had covered the holes in the ground with ferns camouflaging the twelve-foot drop onto razor-sharp spikes. The food supplies also were rigged to kill, if needed. A system was devised by Uncle that would punish anyone who happened across the cabin and decided to raid their stash. A simple storage mantra of *After 5, Stay Alive* was taught to the boys. This meant the first five items on the shelves had been tainted.

Uncle taught the boys about how people had become lazy on the outside and could not produce or supply their own food. They had been trained by society to grab the first thing on the shelf in a store. Tomek and Drake were taught these things about people. They were taught tendencies and baiting techniques about everything, especially humans. The *After 5, Stay Alive* rule meant the boys ate the stored food starting from the back of their supplies.

Uncle's favorite elixir of toxin was readily available in the Michigan woods. A combination of a semi-tall, white, capped mushroom he referred to as "the Death Angel," along with a sweet-smelling dark berry called Nightshade. The mushrooms were not abundant in their area, but when they encountered them, they collected as many as they could carry. Luckily, a little bit went a long way in terms of their intended uses for it. Eating just a sliver of the mushrooms would promptly shut down the liver, kidneys, and stomach organs. In less than two hours, death. Uncle knew the process could be accelerated if it directly entered one's bloodstream.

Nightshade is a tall and bushy plant that grows abundantly throughout their home riverside area. The flowers grow in long clusters, and the berries are purple, black, and flat. The entire plant is poisonous, particularly the roots. The boys knew all too well the damage the poison could do.

Uncle had taught the boys to mix the Nightshade into a stew with river water and boil it overnight. The sugars in the berries would caramelize, and the chemicals would draw out of the fungi, leaving them with a sappy substance of pure, natural, chemical death. The boys remembered clearly seeing it put to use the first time. It was important to Uncle that they learn this lesson firsthand.

Uncle had gone to using this type of poison on each of his arrow tips after shooting an elk one day, many years before, and watching the arrow shaft penetrate deep into the bull's shoulder plate. The bull had taken off and made it closer to civilization than Uncle had liked. As good of a tracker as Uncle was, even he knew he could not find the elk after the shot. He was sure he mortally wounded the prize bull but could not risk tracking it into the small town nearby.

"Taking a life for no reason is wrong," Uncle preached after each kill. He vowed to never again lose an animal he had wounded. "If you take a life, you must make reason of it in order to release the dead's soul."

To make the poison's effectiveness clear to the twins, Uncle trapped a deer in a trail noose designed to hold its prey but not kill it. The boys walked upon her slowly as she thrashed and jumped, trying unsuccessfully to flee the confines of her prison. Uncle struck the deer with a sap-dipped dart from his blowgun in her rear hind quarter.

The doe spun around and dropped to her knees. Looking directly at them, she lay on her side where they could see her chest rise and fall with each breath. Then it happened. Less than three minutes had passed. The Nightshade had instantly frozen her nervous system, as it was designed by nature to do. The toxins brought her to the ground where the Death Angel shut down her organs and she died laying there, staring at the boys.

Those three were the last thing she saw. Uncle often dreamed about that doe. Only in his vivid dreams, the deer could talk. The dream always had the same ending just before he awoke. The doe stops fighting, draws her last breath, looks to him at that moment of death with two spotted fawns behind her and says,

"Take ..."

3 OTHERS

It echoed throughout the valley at daybreak and jolted the boys awake. The clear, crisp rifle blast was unmistakable and not far away. Tomek was first to his feet, bow in hand and quiver on his back. Drake was not far behind with a belt full of throwing knives and his spear. Both boys were ready for battle, clutching their favorite tools of war. As the second shot rang out, they knew the exact location of the trespasser.

"It came from the orchard near the overgrown section near mid-hill," Drake said.

"Probably a wandering hunter," Tomek guessed.

This was not the first time they had been close to strangers in their area. At least a few times each year, a group of outdoorsmen or two would float by on the river. They would often just hide and wait them out. If they were seen, a simple wave was all that was needed. The boys had dressed in army fatigue camouflage every day of their lives. Added to this was a mixture of torn burlap and natural plant life. The boys could drop to the ground and vanish at any point, on any day of the year. To any passerby they were just a part of the landscape. This is how

Uncle taught them to be. However, this time was different. Uncle was not there.

As the hollowed-out tree door opened, both of them knew the situation was worse than they had thought. Both boys looked out to the river and saw it at the same time. The aluminum canoe shimmered in what was left of the past night's moon. Whomever was shooting had landed and beached forty yards from their front door.

How did this happen without them waking? Had they been found? Who was shooting? Drake looked at Tomek and for the first time saw a change in his brother's eyes. Tomek's rage was nothing new. Uncle had seen it in him as well and never corrected it. Tomek was taught to use it as a weapon.

Trying to calm his brother, Drake made sure Tomek would not be in direct contact with the shooter.

"You take the blossom ridge and come down from the hilltop," Drake planned. "I will walk up the river edge and flank to the west."

Tomek agreed.

Both boys had their strengths. When it came to brute strength, agility, and marksmanship, Tomek was Uncle's killing machine. Drake was just as deadly with his knives but was much more calculated, tactical, and could easily outsmart and trap his way into and out of situations. Uncle knew this from the day Drake escaped the hospital and met him at the big pine.

As they separated, Drake walked along the river's edge, utilizing the sound of the babbling river to hide his footsteps. He quickly knew what awaited him downriver as he spotted the dead deer alone on the bank from fifty yards away.

Recognizing the drop from the hillside down to the bank and the path it must've taken before it expired, he knew the hunter was either still on his way down the hill or walking upstream to find a place to safely climb down and retrieve the game. Either way, Drake had time to set up a quick blind utilizing some driftwood and an outcropping of rock. From this spot he would be invisible to anyone coming up to the deer from any location. Drake sat, patiently waiting for his prey to take the bait.

Meanwhile, Tomek quickly stalked his way through the orchard on top of the ridge. Using the height of the ridge to look down upon the valley gave him a great advantage. The gleam caught his eye. An empty .308 shell casing that was still wet with the morning dew was in front of him. Next to it was the hunter's pack and a small area of matted-down grass.

"This is the spot where he killed my deer," Tomek uttered to himself. With an arrow knocked, he walked in the hunter's steps. With each step he fought the racing of his heart and could feel the tightness in his fingers upon the bowstring. Tomek could not remember the last time he had the excitement, the nerves, and the adrenaline of a true hunt.

Tomek worked downhill and was now not only on the hunter's trail, but he had picked up the injured deer's blood trail and spoor. Tomek would be the first of the boys to see the invader. A tall man who seemed to be about ten years older than the boys, wearing camouflage pants and a black over blue flannel shirt. The intruder also adorned a bright orange vest that allowed Tomek to keep his distance but easily see him through the brush. Tomek laughed to himself about the hunter's attire and immediately considered him a lesser outdoorsman and barely even human.

"This trash does not belong in my woods," Tomek said bitterly to himself as he smoothed out the turkey feather fletching on the knocked arrow.

The hunter, oblivious to the fact that he was not alone, stood at the drop off near the bank and admired his kill from above. A perfect eight-point buck, majestic and powerful; a true trophy lay below him. And as Drake had figured, the hunter then made his way down river for about 300 yards until a feasible spot to climb down was found.

Tomek slowly moved to the spot that the hunter vacated once he headed down river to get on the bank. It provided the perfect ambush from above.

24

"Prey feels the safest in places it knows," Tomek remembered Uncle telling him. "Kill him in his home, and he will die without knowing."

Because the hunter had just left the ridge, he most likely would not look up above when he returned to the area. Tomek was right where Uncle would have wanted him to be.

Drake sat motionless until he heard the unmistakable clash of boots in the water fighting against the current. The hunter may as well have been banging pots and pans together as he approached. The blue shirt and orange vest were easy to pick out against the river bank for Drake, as well. Drake was positioned perfectly with the deer between himself and the brightly dressed man. Suddenly, he began to second-guess his trap. At fifteen yards the hunter stopped abruptly, shouldered his gun, and aimed it directly at Drake. Frozen in place, Drake's only hope was that the man was surveying the dead buck to see if it needed a follow-up shot. Drake closed his eyes and tuned in his senses to stay as still as possible.

Click.

The sound of the safety being released could mean only one thing. The hunter was ready to shoot, but what was the hunter going to shoot at? Every inch of his body told him to run, run fast, run away. Yet Uncle's voice in his head told him otherwise.

"Stay, hold tight, trust your surroundings. Be the snake, not the mouse."

Drake sat still with his eyes closed, slowed his heart rate with deep breaths, until he next sound he heard was a familiar one.

Shheeewww …….. thhwwwwaaap!

Drake opened his eyes, surprised to see the hunter on his knees and falling down face-first into the river bank. The arrow had entered behind his right eye at the temple and exited his lower jaw, where it lodged into the clavicle. There was no sound from the hunter as the river turned red with blood from the gaping wound the sharpened, razor-like flint stone head had created.

The world fell silent again, and Drake had never been so happy to have a brother who could shoot like that.

4 DEATH

The boys stood over the hunter, silently surveying the body.

"Who was he?" Drake pondered. *"Why did he come to us? Did he have a family and was he going to shoot me or the deer?"*

"We need to burn him, gut the buck, and send his boat downstream," Tomek said nonchalantly, breaking the silence.

Drake agreed, but it was not what Tomek said that caught his attention. That is, in fact, what Uncle would have told them to do. It was how cold, simple, and calculated it was delivered by Tomek. This man was just an animal to him. Drake did not spend too much time worrying about the change in his brother and laughed to himself, *"At least Tomek does not want to eat him."*

While dragging the carcasses back to their fire pit, Tomek recollected how the stalk through the orchard happened and admitted even he could not see Drake inside the tangles of wood, seaweed, and rocks. Drake realized that Tomek had no idea he was saving his brother's life, and he was not sure if that was a good thing or not. Drake knew that Tomek killing a man to save his own brother is much different than Tomek killing the man just to do it.

"I found his blind and his pack," Tomek said. "It was loaded pretty full. We need to go back and see if there are any supplies we can use. And now we have a gun."

"You know what Uncle said about guns," Drake quickly retorted. His concern was met with a reply that was truer at this moment than any before.

"Well, Uncle is not here, now is he?"

No, he was not there. Yet Drake remembered back to the many talks they had about firearms with Uncle.

"It is better to silently hunt with the disadvantage of a handheld weapon than to easily kill with the blast of a gun," Uncle had said around the fire pit many a night. "There is no honor in killing with a gun."

Until this day, Drake never really realized how true that lesson was. For the simple fact that if the hunter had killed the buck with a bow, the twins would still be sleeping.

The dead hunter's wet clothes weighed him down as the twins turned the river bend just before their camp. Exhausted from the double drag job of both the man and the deer, the boys were not concentrating as they normally would on their stealth. This allowed neither to notice the canoe missing upon their return.

Drake dropped the man at the banks of the river and removed his clothes while Tomek went back to the orchard to retrieve the hunter's pack. They had been taught to utilize as much as they could from a kill, and this would be no different.

"Clothing is not natural and burns different than wood," Uncle would warn them. "Never burn anything that is unnatural. The smell and the color of the smoke could alert someone to your whereabouts. Campfires are often ignored, but trash burn piles never are."

Drake was now hearing Uncle's voice more and more each day as the logic behind the lessons they were taught became abundantly clearer.

The body was covered in driftwood as Drake ignited the tender kindling he had set as a base layer. It did not take long for the warmth of the blaze to radiate on his dark, blood-stained skin. Drake figured Tomek would see the smoke and return soon to enjoy the fire. Kneeling at the river's edge to scoop up some water and begin to rinse his body, he saw Tomek's reflection in the river. Drake anxiously turned around to see what kind of gear his brother had returned with.

Boom!

The bullet grazed Drake's cheek and removed the lower part of his left ear. Drake found himself now lying in the river, flat on his back. He lifted his head and deciphered the blurred figure. The hunter was alive and stood wearing his blue flannel shirt, orange vest, and pants, grasping a shiny silver handgun, which was shaking in his right hand. The hunter yelled at Drake, but Drake could not make out the words. The sound of the running water mixed with an intense ringing in his ears only allowed him to see the hunter's mouth moving. Drake attempted to get up, struggling onto one knee, not knowing for sure if he was dizzy from the shot or if he was already dead.

The feeling of the gun barrel pressed against his temple was one he knew he would never forget, especially if his life was about to end. The cold metal pierced through his hair as it pressed against his skin. He looked down into the river and watched blood run from his ear and cheek and disappear into the current. Drake's hearing partially returned in time to hear the click of the revolver's rolling drum magazine, which seemed surprisingly loud next to his damaged ear.

With the barrel held tight to his head, he could feel the hunter's hand quivering almost uncontrollably. Drake knew now was his moment as he heard Uncle's voice:

"Never close your eyes just before you kill a man; that is the moment when your weakness will be seen. The snake has open eyes when he strikes the mouse!"

Without looking, Drake knew the hunter's eyes were closed. If the hunter was a capable killer, Drake would already be dead. Drake reached to his left ankle under the water and removed the tactical knife from its holster. With his grip firm on the leather-wrapped handle, he rolled forward, swinging his leg down behind the knees of the hunter. In one fluid and fast motion, Drake reached across, grasped the hunter's waist, and pulled him backward over the leg trap. As the hunter fell into the water, the shot rang off.

Boom!

The round fired harmlessly into the sky as Drake looked into the hunter's eyes now from above. Drake kept his eyes open and drove the knife deep into the hunter's heart. He drew the blade from the man's chest in a split second, and as quickly as he felt the knife clear the man's ribs, Drake slashed the man's throat.

Drake pushed the enemy's dangling head underwater to finish him off while standing to his feet. He looked to his left and could make out the vague figure of a second body with his blurred vision. Alongside the fire, wearing the original blue flannel shirt, was Tomek. In the fire was a body, but whose body? Drake knew he had just killed the same man Tomek had shot with the bow. Drake had seen his face close up and looked into his eyes as he died both times.

Tomek walked out into the knee-deep water where Drake stood and took his brother's head to his shoulder. Tomek then spoke softly and directly into his undamaged right ear.

"We killed twins."

5 FLOWS

Sitting by the raging fire with the two bodies for fuel, the twins began to inventory the hunter's pack that was left in the orchard. Plenty of canned food rations, fruit, trail mix and powdered eggs, all of which was quickly burned.

Tomek and Drake survived on their *After 5, Stay Alive* mantra to the extreme. This included not scavenging others' meal supplies. Drake was happy to find knives, both big and small as well, as their matching sheaths. He was particularly fond of the wood-handled six-inch Rapala fillet knife in the pack, knowing that cleaning fish would now be much easier. The rest of the pack contained an assortment of money, deer tags, and ammunition.

Also in the pack was a yellow satellite cellular phone. The twins were aware of phones and the general capabilities they possessed. Uncle had been in the woods so long before the day he found the twins, even he was uneducated about the overall technological power of the small cellular devices.

"This is cool," Tomek said while pushing random buttons on the unit and finding amusement in the different tones it produced. "We should keep it."

"First a gun and now a phone thingy? Really, Tomek?"

Drake was not exactly thrilled about the idea of keeping either item, but he knew what battles to pick and choose when dealing with his brother.

"The rifle we should keep, just in case that bear cub is around again," Drake said, pointing to Tomek's backside.

Two years ago, Tomek had a nasty encounter with a bear cub and Drake relentlessly found pleasure in bringing it up as often as he could. Tomek had landed the cub in a leg hold trap meant for a fox and was trying to set it free when he got a nice claw swipe across his ass cheek. Of course, Tomek was too proud to let his brother care for his butt wounds, leaving him with an infection that would heal but not without leaving quite the scar.

"At least the scar isn't on my face there, ear boy," Tomek snapped back.

"Damn it. Good point," Drake thought to himself, as to not give Tomek any credit for the quick retort.

"If I ever see that bear again, I am going to use this rifle and shoot him in the ass!" Tomek quipped as both boys laughed.

It was the first time they had smiled together since Uncle's death. Tomek soon grew bored with the yellow beeping cell phone and tossed it into the river.

"Time to crush some bones," Tomek said with a sigh. It was the first time Drake heard his brother speak negatively regarding any process of the killing of the hunters. Of course, he figured it was more about the fact that they now had some actual work to do.

34

The scorched bones were pulled from the fire pit and placed one by one onto a large, flat riverside boulder they often referred to as the whale rock, due to its shape and how it emerged from the water line. Not that either boy had ever seen a whale, but Uncle explained the way they breached the water in order to breathe from their blow holes. Drake, as a child, had drawn a face on it with a piece of sodium limestone mixed with crushed mulberries. Uncle sternly made him stand in the chest deep forty-degree water the next day to wash it off. A cold lesson learned.

The boys took turns dropping the heaviest rocks they could find onto the bones, piece by piece. Breaking them up into unrecognizable flakes and tossing them into the river. With one rib bone left, Tomek stopped his brother.

"This one is mine," Tomek said, picking up the black and grey charcoal-covered rib. "My trophy."

Drake rolled his eyes, knowing that Tomek was always the one who cared about antlers on a deer or the size of a fish. He guessed this kill was no different. Tomek had to have his trophy.

The next morning, they awoke and enjoyed their pancake griddle breakfast with some blueberries they had collected back in the late summer. It was a quiet September morning with the perfect amount of crispness in the air. The summer months were ending, and the last fly hatch of the year was about to happen, meaning the day would be spent trout fishing and smoking the meat to preserve it for the bitter winter months ahead.

The next few weeks the twins spent nearly every minute of the day
together. The schedule of separating tasks was dropped and both
agreed on what the day's activities would be. This time of the year the
twins were much like a bear before hibernation, gathering food and
putting on fat for the long sleep ahead. The corn was to be picked, as
well as the last of the other summer vegetables. This included canning
what was to be saved. The orchards were full of fruit that was picked
and enjoyed by both equally.

Hundreds of pounds of apples were stored in the underground
cellar. The cool temperature underground kept the stash from spoiling.
A fresh crisp apple could be had on a cold January day. It was always
one of the few bright spots during the dreary days of winter. Fresh
apples and corn were also the best winter baits for their deer pit traps.
Every year, multiple deer fell into the pits attempting to feast on the
small bounty of apples the twins had laid out for them on top of the
false fern-covered floor surrounding the main garden.

Life went on quietly and peacefully with no hunters, intruders, or
even many flyovers, which was unusual. They had figured that
eventually a search party would have come looking for the two "lost"
hunters. Having worked out their backstory if someone came to their
camp, both could easily deny any knowledge of the hunters. Both boys
planned on helping in the search efforts if need be in order to cast away
any light that may draw suspicions their way. It was a peaceful winter.
They figured the daily snowfalls and ice rain mix had kept the search
parties away from their section of woods. Not a single hunter, trapper

or even plane was seen in their area until spring and that's the way they liked it.

The snow came quickly and heavily that year. By the end of November, they were completely buried in more than three feet. December came and went. The only reminder of Uncle's death was the fried bluegill fillets they dined on that night. It was his favorite meal. Soon they began to hear the daily cracking of the ice floes in the river. Only the first eight-foot portion of each side of the sixty-foot-wide waterway froze solid enough to support the boys' weight. Tomek and Drake could always count on open water and cold fishing, if need be.

Spring came just as it did every year with the breaking of the river ice. It was quite a powerful and magical thing to see. Every ice chunk that came from upstream would eventually pile into huge ice jams along the front of their bend in the river. The jams would stick around every year for about a week, and then slowly make their way downstream. The left behind plenty of fresh gouges in the riverbank and shorelines, much like a glacier carving out an entire continent. The ice floes were so heavy this year that the path of the river had changed, and now the whale rock was completely underwater. The ice floes would also leave items behind that the boys found useful. Logs for building or burning, random eating utensils, hand tools, fishing rods, and even camp stoves often would wash downstream and not make it past their bend.

The river often had a way of bringing them what they needed in terms of food and supplies. It also disposed of what they didn't need, such as the bones of a hunter or two. It was what they did not need that would soon matter to them the most. Many months after the fact, and thirteen miles downriver in Pine Run, a small lumber mill town, what they thought they didn't need showed up on top on an ice floe.

A child playing on the ice floes that had come ashore grabbed it having no idea exactly what it was and took it right to her father. The girl's father, being the local sheriff, knew exactly what it was and had a good idea on who it might have belonged to. The sheriff's notions were confirmed the minute he read the label on the back: *Property of the United States Department of Justice.*

Tomek had no clue that the waterproof satellite phone would have made it this far. He had no clue the batteries would have survived through the winter in the river. There was no way for either Tomek or Drake to know that the hunters were the sons of a high-ranking government official. There was no way for them to know that the hunters were promising college star athletes. Most of all, Tomek could not have known that the phone tracked its coordinates via GPS.

The hunters' disappearance was a national news story. Both from a political standpoint with a powerful father, as well as on the athletic front. Multiple rescue parties were dispatched, only they were fifteen miles to the west of the where the hunters took their last breaths. The snow and ice conditions of the following winter had stopped the search parties from getting any closer. With the discovery of the phone and its data now downloaded, the parties could resume their search efforts utilizing the GPS tracking software. This in effect would put them in the twins' orchard. The track would continue down the hill, then into the river. It was out of pure luck that Tomek never took the phone directly to the cabin.

Not only did the phone give insight to the last known locations of the lost hunters, there also were four photos saved to its internal memory card. The sheriff, an outdoorsman himself, knew the hunters could not have survived that hard of a winter, but he still was shocked as he flipped through the stored images. The first picture featured the hunters together in their camp. The next picture was of the dead buck lying below on the river bed.

The sheriff then looked in horror at the third image, which clearly showed hunter number one's naked body in a pile of brush with an arrow through his head and chest. The sheriff now knew that the government official's sons were not just "lost."

The last photograph on the memory card confirmed his suspicions. The same sheriff, who had investigated the disappearance of two three-year-old twins thirteen years ago, was now looking at the picture of a sixteen-year-old dark skinned wild-eyed killer. Tomek had given them his face without even knowing it. The twins were about to get some company.

6 PINE RUN

The sheriff sat at his desk pondering his next move. The small town of Pine Run, where he was born and raised, had just settled back into normalcy as the attention drawn to it from the missing hunters had hardly subsided over time. The twins who died at the hands of Tomek and Drake were the sons of a United States Congressman. Not only adding political flair to the case, but both hunters also happened to be star athletes on their respective collegiate baseball teams; both were expected to be taken in the next season's Major League draft. Their disappearance was national news, and it thrust Pine Run into the national spotlight for all the wrong reasons.

The sheriff was not looking forward to pushing the residents back into the national news with a now confirmed single—and possibly double—homicide case. Turning the information he had over to the Department of Justice, or even the state troopers, meant he would not be involved in the investigation or be given any credit in regard to capturing the killer. That was something the sheriff's ego would not let happen.

Pine Run was usually a quiet town where the locals relied on the logging and milling industries, as well as a handful of artisan shops, to drive the small economy. One grocery store and one general hardware store were all that was needed. Both let customers run tabs and pay their bills at the end of the month. It was a small and trusting town. The hospital was just as small, but it served the area well. Although, history had shown they did lose a child patient about eight years ago.

Pine Run had another bustling dark economy hidden away from the general public's eyes. Narcotics. Due to its heavily wooded trails, river access to the Great Lakes, and its proximity to the Canadian borders, Pine Run was a central hub for prescription drug runners coming in from abroad and working their way down through Saginaw toward Flint and Detroit. Having a police force that was almost completely in on the take and paid off by the dealers did not help the situation one bit.

The day Drake snuck away under his watch was the day the town had lost faith in the sheriff. He remained on the job, but the town residents generally had little need for him. Only his ego and the large amount of drug money in his bank accounts kept him in the small town. When it came down to actual law enforcement, if there was a problem in Pine Run, his deputies handled it and normally handled it well.

The residents' views on the sheriff were based on the fact that he had not solved the only two big cases in Pine Run's last sixteen years. The original disappearance of the twins and their mother, combined with the hospital losing Drake, were both situations that loomed over his career reputation. To the town, the sheriff was a joke. Not only as an investigator, but as a law enforcement official in general. The story of how the sheriff was high on pain medication, hit an elk in his patrol car, and then drove it right into the middle of the closed laundromat is a town favorite when discussing the man in charge of keeping them all safe.

With all this weighing on his mind, the answer to his dilemma was clear. The sheriff and his deputies must be the ones to find the bodies of the hunters. He took it upon himself and his men to hunt down the killer and bring him to justice. Only then did he feel that the respect due to him would finally be granted.

With his decision made, all that was left to do was pack up his gear and inform his rag tag group of four deputies that they were headed to the woods for a week of survival training. Two of them were ex-military, and the other two were experienced in the outdoors, so the sheriff knew they wouldn't mind a week or so to get out of the town and into the woods. The sheriff knew he would eventually have to tell them what they were hunting for. To prevent any leaks, he decided to hold that info until they were away from Pine Run. None of them had a clue or even dreamed that it would be for a teenage killer.

Deputy Jack Coleman, who knew nothing about the dirty drug dealings, was in charge of rounding up the weapons, gear, and rations they would need. Though he was a clean cop when it came to the law, Coleman was a complete chauvinist and overall disrespectful person. A former Army infantry second lieutenant, Coleman had seen his fair share of action off the grid in the Middle East. Standing tall at 6-foot-5 and 260 pounds, Deputy Coleman was a force to be reckoned with. His broad shoulders, sandy blonde hair, blue eyes, and block-shaped head would have made Coleman the model of a professional football linebacker. The sheriff often said that Coleman could break up a bar fight by walking in the door.

Deputy Magee, while not nearly the size of Coleman, was twice as experienced. Magee had come from the bustling collegiate areas of down state after serving as a Chief of Police. Having served as a federal agent prior to that around the globe, Magee was by far over qualified to be working in Pine Run. Yet, the small town is where he retired. Eventually the boredom grew, and he joined the Sheriff's Department for something to do. Magee quickly became the sheriff's right-hand man, and he was also the group's top marksman. Deputy Ken Magee was at his best when he was aiming down the barrel or scope of a gun. The often soft spoken Magee could be worked up into frenzy with a simple ribbing if the topic of his sister came up. Being that she was married to the sheriff, the guys had plenty of ammunition when it came to ragging on Magee. However, none of them ever questioned his shooting abilities or situational judgment.

One night, after his shift had ended, Deputy Coleman was ambushed and knocked unconscious while walking out to his car in the small parking lot behind the station. The attacker was a known small-time drug dealer out of Flint, Michigan, who did not appreciate Coleman arresting him previously while working his way down from the Canadian border with load of prescription drugs.

The dealer was able to pattern Coleman with inside information provided to him by the sheriff after his arraignment. Having been arrested, the sheriff was worried he might start talking and turn states evidence against the Pine Run Police. The dealer knew way too much as far as the sheriff was concerned. The sheriff had figured Coleman would easily take out the dealer upon being attacked, however that is not what happened.

Coleman awoke confused and dreary to the sight of Magee with his pistol drawn and aiming directly at him from twenty-five feet away. Struggling, it was only then that Coleman realized he was being used as a human shield, and his assailant had a gun to his head.

"Take one more step, pig, and I'll blow his head off, man," the strung-out dealer threatened.

Magee continued talking while stepping forward; addressing both Coleman and the gunman at the same time. Working his way in closer and closer, speaking calmly in a low conversational tone, Magee knew situations like this all too well. Magee knew that the gunman would not fire while he was speaking to him. His training had made it clear that the gunman would only shoot to make a point and would do it at the end of a sentence. Magee took one last step forward, and in the middle of speaking, he pulled the trigger.

It was over as soon as it began for Coleman. He recalled seeing the flash and then suddenly standing alone. Magee had fired and killed the man holding Coleman captive from a distance of seventeen feet with one shot. Coleman turned to see the drug dealer dead on the ground with a bullet entry wound directly in the center of his forehead. The Army veteran knew instantly at that moment that Magee's round was less than two inches from killing him. He was never so glad that Ken Magee was the one who had pulled the trigger, and Magee was glad that the dealer was dead.

The title of biggest hunter in the group would belong to the only female deputy in the history of the Pine Run Sheriff's Department.

Deputy Annette Henderson was born to hunt, trap, and fish. Henderson, the other clean cop, also served as the department's detective. Unlike her male counterparts, she was able to defuse situations and solve investigations by just talking with people. Deputy Henderson utilized these skills and never failed to get a job for which she applied. She excelled not only at being interviewed but also interviewing people. Every suspect Henderson arrested personally thanked her. The sheriff often jokingly attributed it to Henderson using hypnosis, to which Henderson would reply with her personal motto, "It is not what you ask, it is how you ask it." Deputy Henderson used not only her skills as a hunter and investigator, but also her womanly charm and good looks to become a master of manipulation.

Having moved away from Pine Run as a child, this place was the first home she knew. Her mother was a drug addict, which led to a bitter divorce, and her father moved downstate years ago. Taking her with him, she only visited Pine Run in the summers when school was out. Only a few visits ever happened because of a fight between her parents in regard to her mother being high and not caring for Henderson.

Henderson's father never allowed her to visit Pine Run again, and she lost contact with her mother for many years. Upon graduation from college, she knew Pine Run was the place she wanted to live in an attempt to straighten out a big piece of her life that was missing all those years.

Anthony Ravizza, a K-9 Deputy, rounded out the group. Other than Coleman, Ravizza was the only one with actual military experience. He was never in combat like his deputy brethren, but he was directly responsible for getting many warriors out of hostile zones and home safe. Having originally been in the Air Force, he was quickly promoted up to Special Forces as an orienteering instructor. Ravizza taught all the Special Forces units in every branch of the government how to operate off the grid. Ravizza specialized in using nothing but the stars and sun as a guide. Adding a map and compass to his arsenal effectively made him a human GPS. For a man who was never lost, Ravizza ended up in Pine Run for just that reason.

While still in the service, he was stationed at the Air Force base just a few counties away from Pine Run in Oscoda. While training on a night operation in the nearby national forest, he became lost. Having no map or compass, he looked to the stars and moon to guide him. Even in cases of a cloud-covered sky, Ravizza could use the dim brightness of the lingering moon as a guide. Only this evening there were no clouds, and the moon had given way to Michigan's famous Northern Lights.

Ravizza quickly learned afterward that, scientifically speaking, the Northern Lights, or *Aurora Borealis,* is a natural light display in the sky, particularly in high-latitude regions. It is caused by the collision of energetically charged particles with atoms in the high-altitude atmosphere. Being from Southern California, he knew nothing of this glowing effect that covered the sky in waving streaks of green, purple, and red.

That night in northern Michigan was the first time Ravizza had ever felt lost. The first time he had ever succumbed to the power of Mother Nature. Having no clue where he was, what way to go, or what to do left Ravizza with a sense of freedom he had never known. The feeling was so profound to him that upon retirement, he found the area best known for its Northern Lights and started a new life there. That town just happened to be Pine Run.

A federal grant provided the department with a drug dog not long after the attack on Coleman. The drug runners increasingly traversed through the area from Canada using the old logging roads and game trails. The sheriff chose Ravizza as the recipient of the dog, not only because Ravizza was on the take with the sheriff, but the sheriff reasoned, "If the damn mutt runs away, Ravizza is the one who will be able to find it." When it was time to choose a name for his four-legged partner, Ravizza settled on naming her after the reason he was in Pine Run in the first place – the Northern Lights. He had also always liked the Roman goddess of dawn, Aurora.

With his team of deputies set to go, the sheriff and his crew headed deep into the woods as far as their off-road utility vehicles could take them. From there, only the sheriff knew that it would be a seventeen-mile hike through the dense pine, oak, and birch forests to the reach the last place the yellow satellite phone had marked its known location. The squad was headed for the twin's hillside orchard.

7 MOWGLI

As they trudged down a leaf-covered hill in a section of tall oak trees, whose fallen acorns resembled marbles under their feet, the deputies grew impatient with the so-called training exercise.

"What the hell?" Coleman complained. "We have been hiking for hours, and it is starting to get dark."

"What's the matter, big boy? Can't keep up?" Henderson remarked, strolling past Coleman along the trail as he bent over to catch his breath.

"Oh, I can keep it up, all right," Coleman sneered back. "Why don't you climb in my sleeping bag and find out tonight, sweetie?"

Coleman's relentless sexual harassment continued toward Henderson, as always.

"Sorry, I am not into bestiality. I don't hook up with pigs like you," Henderson retorted.

"Oink, oink, baby," Coleman responded, tilting his head back to lift his nose up like a swIne.

"Since we're in the woods, it might be the perfect time for some jungle fever, huh, Coleman?" Ravizza chimed in, poking at the fact Henderson was black.

"Mmmm, yeah, a little dark meat might be on the menu," Coleman offered.

"Why don't you just shut your damn mouth for once and follow orders?" Magee suggested.

"Oh, well, thanks for the suggestion. I will definitely take it into consideration once our fearless Boy Scout leader up there admits that he hasn't told us jack ..."

"Shit?" the sheriff answered from the front of the line.

"Yeah, jack shit," Coleman replied.

"No ... bear shit," Henderson said, pointing down at the ground under Coleman with a massive smile on her face. "Not jack shit. Bear shit, as in you're standing in it."

The group all busted out laughing as Coleman vigorously rubbed the bottoms of his ragged, worn-out boots in the nearby grass. They found enjoyment in his kicking motion as he attempted to remove as much of the bear's processed lunch as he could.

"Hey Coleman, if the bear's name was also Jack, then you're right. It is Jack shit!" Magee added, piling on to Coleman's boot situation.

"Well, I guess that answers that age-old question," Ravizza added.

"What question?" Coleman asked, his tone lightening up, seeing the humor in the situation.

"Bears really do shit in the woods!"

The entire group continued laughing at the expense of Jack Coleman again, and he stood there confused, not familiar with why anyone would ever wonder such a dumb thing.

"Shut up, Air Force boy," Coleman said. He found something about everyone to use as ammunition when it came to insults. The fact that he was combat infantry and Ravizza was not just added to it.

"You're not half the cop I am, Ravizza!" Coleman continued.

"Look at your block head and big fat ass, Coleman," Ravizza struck back. "I am literally ... half the cop you are, piggy."

Coleman had the same comeback for him as he did a few minutes earlier while being called a member of the swine family. While looking at Henderson and Ravizza, he gave each of them a distinctive "Oink, oink."

"All right, it's time to set camp and debrief," the sheriff said, dropping his hiking frame pack from his back, effectively killing the moment.

"Do I get to debrief Henderson?" Coleman again tried to focus the target of laughter away from him.

"You are still, and never will be, my type," she replied.

"Not without surgery anyway," the sheriff quipped.

This comment was met with a glaring stare from Henderson directly at him. There had been many times when he had publicly outed her in this way. As her boss, she felt he constantly crossed way over the line. The sheriff knew Henderson was gay and had openly told her behind closed doors that reporting or filing a complaint against him would mean her having to come out to the rest of the world, something she was not yet ready to do at that point in her life.

Most everyone in the small town knew she was gay and did not care. Yet Henderson felt that Pine Run was not like the rest of the world, and that is why she had decided to live there away from her family in Fenton in the first place.

"All right, let's get this fire going. We still have about six miles to cover at first light."

"Sleeping here, huh?" Ravizza asked.

"This spot is as good as any," Henderson said, bending over to drop her hiking pack and supply bag.

The motion of her bending over in front of the guys did not go unnoticed. Just about every one of them silently enjoyed the view, tilting their heads to the side in relation to the angle at which she bent.

"Lord have mercy," Coleman said.

"We should probably leave the Lord out of it," Ravizza replied in a joking tone.

"Bless me, Father, for I have sinned," Coleman added.

Magee playing the part of the preacher and jumped right in. "And what are these sins you wish to be absolved of, my son?"

"Coveting my neighbor's possessions," Coleman said.

"That is not exactly what is meant by coveting, my son," Magee said.

"Well, Father, she possesses that booty, and I want it!" Coleman replied.

"Anything else, my child?" Magee asked, keeping up the charade.

"Adultery, coveting her possessions, and did I mention adultery?" Coleman said, still enjoying the view that Henderson was unknowingly presenting to him.

"Adultery, huh? And when did you commit these acts?" Father Magee asked.

"I haven't yet," Coleman answered.

Coleman's frat boy-like confident attitude in regard to actually being able to woo Henderson in anyway whatsoever made the rest of the group roll their eyes. It was about this time that Henderson caught on to exactly what was happening behind her back. Having listened for a brief second, she decided she wanted to ruin the moment for them, and Mother Nature had provided her with the perfect opportunity.

Bending back over and running her hands downward from her lower back in a sensual manner, she stopped them on her butt. Henderson turned her head back slowly to look at them and flicked her pony tail up and over the other side of her face. Making eye-to-eye contact, she looked Coleman directly in the eyes, made a kissing gesture with her lips, and let loose the biggest fart that any of them had ever heard come out of a woman.

The campsite exploded with laughter, and the guys knew they had been had. It was moments like this that kept Henderson from leaving the department. She could handle the harassment and was always one step ahead of the men.

"You just shit on me while I was in confession," Magee said.

"Sorry Father, but I guess that makes it a holy shit," Henderson said, again one step ahead of them, even with jokes. The softer mood of their joking carried on while they continued to set the camp and prepare their meals.

With camp set and their stomachs filled to the brim, the topic of conversation turned back into their so-called training mission.

"Now, I'm sure you're all wondering why the hell I have dragged you out here," the sheriff said. The group sat, nodding in silence, waiting on what was to follow.

"I will admit I have not been honest with you guys," the sheriff started. "This is not a training mission; it's a manhunt. Well, a boy hunt," he said, removing the yellow satellite phone from his frame pack.

"My daughter found this phone, and it has four pictures on it. One of them is the last known picture taken of the Senator's sons who went missing last year."

Flipping through the images one by one, he gave them the play by play of what they were seeing.

"Here is a nice buck one of them must have shot ..."

Henderson being the biggest hunter in the group was the most interested in this one.

"And here is one of the brothers dead ... with a fucking arrow through his skull."

The sheriff spoke with little emotion while showing the picture and passing the phone around to the task force he had assembled.

Each member of the party examined the phone's photos, and the mood around the campfire suddenly transformed. Before tonight, they all had enough sense to know that the twin hunters were most likely dead. Not a single one of them ever imagined they would one day be looking at picture showing one of the brothers murdered.

"So, we are looking for a dead man and his missing brother?" Magee asked.

"No, we are looking for a dead man, his missing brother, and whoever the hell this teenage kid covered in blood is," Ravizza added, clicking over to the next image.

Magee, being the highest seniority deputy behind the sheriff, looked at the picture and immediately recognized the face.

"Holy hell, its Mowgli!"

The nickname was given to Drake upon his stay in the hospital all those years ago in reference to Rudyard Kipling's *The Jungle Book*, where a child is raised in the wild by animals. Though the picture was of Tomek and not Drake, no one knew back in the hospital days, just as they did not know now, that there are actually two Mowglis.

"That is exactly what I am thinking," the sheriff agreed.

"Wait, that's all true?" Coleman seemed confused again. "I thought that was just some story you all told to cover up losing the kid."

With a defensive tone, his boss replied, "Of course it is true. What is it about me that makes you think I would just make something like that up?"

"Well, if the boot fits ..." Coleman had gone out on an accusatory limb, but after all, the sheriff had lied to get them all out there in the first place.

"Well, the boot may fit in your eyes, but at least my boot ain't got bear shit on it!"

Silence ... silence ... HAHAHAHAHAHAHAHA

The mood was again lightened, and the group went into the plans for the remainder of the hike. Sheriff sat with Ravizza going over the GPS data and the maps as Coleman cleaned his boots off – again.

"Damn it. This bear crap soaked through, and it's on my socks," Coleman said, tossing a crusty shit-soaked sock into the fire, much to the displeasure of the noses belonging to those around him.

The group refocused one more time as the sheriff and Ravizza informed them of the general route they would take in the morning and at what time they would be leaving. They tucked into their bags around the warm, flickering glow of the fire. The snaps and pops of the boiling sap inside the pieces of pine mixed with the distant drone of the running river made for a perfect night to be in the woods.

Ravizza rolled over, pulling Aurora close to him. Looking up, he enjoyed being away from the city lights and used the moment to take in the bounty of stars that only northern Michigan can supply. Glancing to the south, he became uneasy, as a large swath of Northern Lights was headed their way and would soon cover them for most of the night. Aurora sensed his uneasiness and whimpered.

"Shhhh, lay down girl," he comforted her, again rubbing the back of her neck and around her rib cage. Within minutes, the nightly cricket ballad mixed with the sounds of the fire, and the roaring of Coleman's giant-sized nostrils filled the air were the only things to be heard.

Though they were quiet now, the damage had been done. The deputies' earlier chorus of laughs and trudging throughout the woods had carried straight down the river valley and alerted the twins that they again were not alone in the woods. Drake was hesitant to go on the offensive, wanting to wait them out, hoping they were just hikers passing through the area. That was until he smelt the burning of Coleman's sock in the air. Drake immediately smirked, thinking back on the times Uncle had said, "Campfires are often ignored, but trash burn piles never are."

Now Drake knew that was truer than ever.

The twins estimated the approximate location of the fire and knew they had to hike a good amount through the dark. Gathering supplies quickly, they loaded the backpack they had scavenged off of the hunters and headed out. Three hours later, the twins found the group. With just embers glowing in the fire, the twins climbed a nearby oak tree for a better observation point.

"Five sleeping bags, guns everywhere," Tomek mouthed silently to his brother.

Drake agreed with the assessment, adding that every coat sported badges. Drake and Tomek knew they were now dealing with the type of people Uncle had warned them about. Not knowing what part of the "government" these intruders represented was not an issue. All that mattered is they were government, and that was enough to eliminate them. Even if they were doing so in Uncle's honor, it was the right thing to do in their minds.

While sitting in the tree sixty yards away from the sleeping intruders, they devised their plan. Tomek would stay back at twenty yards using his bow on the three bags closest to him. Drake would stalk up and wait for Tomek's first shot. While the intruders' focus was on where in the dark the arrows were coming from, Drake would use his throwing knives and eliminate any left standing.

The plan seemed simple and had little risk to the twins. However, their entire outlook on the situation changed instantly when Tomek spoke to his brother, this time clear and out loud,

"They have a wolf."

8 WOLF

Sitting in the canopy of the oak tree amongst the growing acorns and unrelenting mosquitoes, Drake clearly heard what his brother had said. Like many of the other obstacles they faced, Uncle's voice was there with them as they pondered what to do.

"A wolf is a hunter, a killer, and yet still a pack animal. When you find one alone, you must kill it before he can tell the pack where you are. Just like a pack of wolves, you two must fight and hunt together. Alone you are weak; together you are unstoppable. Never fight a pack of wolves. Separate them and take them out, one by one."

When Tomek looked upon the group, he saw a wolf, unlike his brother, Drake. Drake, thinking more broadly, saw a pack.

"I'll shoot the wolf first. Once it's gone, we can take on the rest," Tomek said.

Drake knew that shooting a wolf would not be a silent matter. That was the difference between killing an animal and a man. A man dies in silence, scared of his fate and in shock. Drake knew the wolf would howl and scream upon being hit with the arrow and alert the rest of the deputies in the pack, making them much harder to eliminate.

"I have a better idea," Drake informed Tomek while pulling a jar of honey out his backpack.

Seeing the jar, Tomek smiled. Immediately, he knew his brother's plan was the perfect solution. Uncle had killed a black bear this way once after it continued to invade the garden night after night. The old bear's skin was so thick, Uncle's stone arrowhead would hardly penetrate the bruin's hide. So, like Uncle before them, they knew the rule of *After 5, Stay Alive* was going to come into play.

With his brother's approval, Drake climbed down with the Nightshade and Death Angel tainted honey jar and his steady accompaniment of knives in tow. The deputies foolishly had set camp right along a narrow dirt-packed game trail. The absence of fallen leaves and gravel from the cleared trail allowed Drake a silent approach. Ignoring the clouds of mosquitoes whirling around his head and humming in his ears, he dropped to the ground at thirty yards.

Crawling hand over hand, he was now at ten yards. With the constant light show put on by the green illuminated fireflies, his darkness-adjusted eyes combined with the flickering glow of what was left of the fire made it bright as daylight to him. This was the point of no return, and Drake had to decide whether to step over the sleeping deputies to get close enough to the wolf or to work his way around the outside of the still-sleeping pack. Working his way around the outside meant leaving the hard-packed trail and the possibility of waking the pack as his steps crunched on the forest floor. Knowing that if even a single wolf was to wake up he would be in trouble, Drake chose the riskier but silent route.

The fire sat aglow with embers as Drake approached the first bag. Thankfully, the smoke from the fire had removed most of the mosquitoes from the camp area, and Drake could utilize his full concentration without being bothered. Sleeping on his back with a monstrous snoring roar, Drake approached the sleeping bag of what looked to be a giant. Compared to his sixteen-year-old frame, Drake had never seen a man of Deputy Coleman's size. He also could not believe the others somehow remained asleep through the sound of the snoring giant. While stepping over Coleman's wide waist, he could not help but giggle to himself as the deputy did his best impersonation of a black bear's mating roar. Two more bags of sleeping enemies stood between Drake and Aurora.

Henderson, on her side, was a quick hop over and much easier to get by than the previous bear he had just passed due to the sheer size difference between the two. Looking back to ensure the pack was still asleep, he stood over Henderson. Something was different. Not only did Drake recognize the body as being smaller, but there was something else. There was something about her face that drew him in.

What was it? he wondered. Why was this human different? He quickly realized why as he got closer and closer, now down on one knee. Henderson was a woman. Of course, Uncle had warned them about the dangers of these creatures, but Drake had secretly always disagreed with Uncle on this aspect of human nature. Drake remembered clearly the only woman he had ever talked to. The only dark-skinned person he had ever seen besides himself and Tomek. The nurse from all those years ago. Something about Henderson reminded him of the nurse. While he could not explain his instant infatuation, he was excited to tell Tomek about it upon his return.

Still waiting, Tomek watched from his perch with an arrow knocked and instantly grew angry with his brother, who was now six feet from the sleeping wolf and down on his knee staring into the face of a sleeping target.

"What is he doing?"

Tomek's anger began to boil. Growing impatient with his brother's sudden enchantment, Tomek drew his bow, feeling the tension in his back as he held the string at full draw. He aimed directly over his brother's shoulder. Tomek saw his brother draw in closer to Henderson, and his decision was made. Releasing the grip on his fingers holding back the string, it drug across his bare cheek propelling the arrow downrange, where it directly impacted the middle of the fire pit.

With sparks and embers flying into the air from the arrow's thud-like landing, Drake jumped up and peered into the darkness. At that moment, two thoughts crossed his mind: *"What in the hell is Tomek doing shooting at me?"* and *"Where in the hell is he?"*

Both thoughts continually ran through his head as he stared into the darkness. He knew that if not for the wolf being present, their original plan would have worked perfectly. All five of the targets would have been eliminated easily from the darkness. Even knowing what tree Tomek was in, Drake could not see his brother.

"The wolf!" Drake heard the words escape from the night.

Taking heed to his brother's sudden warning, he slowly spun around, relieved to see all the deputies still sleeping, none the wiser about the arrow's now prominent presence standing tall up on end in the fire pit. His relief quickly evaporated not by what he saw, but by what he heard next.

The low toned, guttural growl was not like one he had heard before. Different and somehow more intimidating than a bear or even a coyote, Aurora was awake. Looking directly at Drake with hunched shoulders, the hair on her back rose like some sort of medieval beast waiting to attack. Drake knew he was in trouble. Reaching for a knife slowly only made things worse as Aurora stepped forward showing her teeth. Drake knew that running was useless, and even if he did make it to a spot where he could climb, the rest of the pack would have him trapped like a cat stuck in a tree.

Drake looked again to the darkness with hope that another arrow would find its way into the circle of sleeping men and kill the wolf holding him silently captive. He plead with his eyes silently into the abyss for help, but there was no arrow. Much like the moment when he was in the river with a gun to his head, Drake was alone in a fight with his brother standing by doing nothing.

"Aurora, lay down you stupid mutt!" the sheriff demanded, without rolling over to see exactly why she was growling. Aurora held her position while taking her intent gaze off of Drake to look over at the sheriff. Much like the moment with the hunter in the river, Drake relied on one of Uncle's teachings again.

"Never close your eyes just before you kill a man. That is the moment when your weakness will be seen. The snake has open eyes when he strikes the mouse"

Using the break in the wolf's concentration, Drake reached down to his right cargo pocket and tossed the contents to the ground. The jar of honey now lay open in between him and the dog. With a great sense of relief, Drake watched as she lowered her head, sniffing the sweetness of the jar. The opening was big enough for Aurora's snout. Feverishly, the dog buried her attention into getting every last drop of the deadly gold bee syrup from out of the jar.

The wolf was now ignoring Drake, and he slipped away from the group and exited back down the path where he originally entered the camp. Stepping back over the still bear-like snoring of Coleman, he looked back and saw the arrow still sticking up in the now extinguished fire pit. Drake walked back toward the pit, grabbed the half-broken cedar arrow shaft at the fletching, and quickly made his exit again over Coleman and back down the trail.

Drake did not go far into the woods. He wanted to stay hidden and watch to make sure the tainted jar of death did its work on the wolf. Making his way back up into a tree twenty yards from the camp, Tomek joined him. They shared a glance, and Tomek knew he was in for a chewing, but that would have to wait. He looked at Drake, shrugged his shoulders, and in a simple attempt to compliment and flatter some of the anger out of Drake said, "I knew you were fine. You always figure your own way out."

Aurora finished what she could of the jar and laid back down next to Ravizza. The twins knew all too well what would happen next. If only a small dipped dart could take down a deer, the entire jar would be more than enough to kill not only a single dog, but the whole pack if need be.

Within five minutes, Aurora started whimpering and rolling on the ground, waking up Ravizza with a constant pawing at his back.

"What's wrong, girl?" he asked, holding her tight as she lay in his lap shivering. Seeing the jar laying on the ground in the early morning sunrise, he asked the group loud enough to wake them all up, "What is this jar, which one of you gave this to her?"

Coleman, who had packed all the food provisions for the group, examined the jar. "I didn't bring this." Smelling it, he added, "We have no use for honey on this trip." Coleman took a swab of the sticky honey on his finger and again held it to his nose. "Yup, honey," he shrugged, opening his mouth.

The twins watched and were ecstatic as Coleman's finger moved towards his mouth to taste the death syrup. Neither of them had figured the giant would be this easy to take out of the pack. A two-for-one kill was the best possible outcome.

Tomek looked at Drake and whispered, "The big bear has to eat big meals."

"Nooooo!"

"Put it down, you damn block-headed fool!" Henderson yelled

while springing across the camp slamming into Coleman. Because of his size, he didn't move from the impact that flung her to the ground. However, her jarring hit was enough to make him question the substance, and he wiped his finger off on his pant leg.

"So close," Drake said disappointingly.

After the ruckus, the group's attention focused back on the now dying K-9 lying in Ravizza' lap. With tears on his face, he held onto his German Shepherd partner, pleading for her to recover and come back to him. The twins knew she was not coming back, but were impressed with how long she had lasted thus far. Still struggling to breathe, the dog remained in Ravizza's grasp, lying there with her outstretched tongue. Suddenly, the dog again began to convulse.

"No, why? No, she is all I have left. No, why?" Ravizza sobbed more unintelligible words in his moment of panicking grief, not caring who could see or hear him. The rest of the group, stunned and saddened at the outpouring of emotion coming from their brother in arms, stood by solemnly.

It was something in the way Ravizza poured over the imminent death of the wolf that struck Drake. Until now, death was just death. No sadness, no joy, just death. Drake watched the grief on Ravizza's face first with amazement, then with a modicum of his own sadness. *"What must it be like to feel for something like that?"*

Drake had never felt that way when Uncle died. He was gone and that was all. Drake even ran through the idea of losing his brother. The only emotion that arose was anger at the thought of having to do all of the survival, hunting, trapping, and garden work by himself. Watching Ravizza cry over his now-suffering dog did stir up emotions in Drake. He did not feel sorry for the wolf. The wolf had to die. He did feel pain and some form of sorrow for Ravizza. Both Tomek and Drake had seen enough and climbed down the back side of the large oak out of sight from the deputies still all standing there watching.

Aurora's chest raised and lowered, shaking with each lift of her rib cage. Whimpering as she exhaled each time through her now completely dry nose, Ravizza looked into her brown eyes. Glassed over and lifeless, not focusing back on her owner, the irises seemed empty. Rubbing his thumb over her head and looking into her eyes, Ravizza felt like her soul was gone. Aurora's soul may have left her body, but the whimpering and crying not only remained but grew louder and more desperate.

Drake looked back one more time to see the rest of the group now packing their gear, no longer watching Aurora's feeble struggle to hold on to life. Everyone had gone, except Ravizza and Henderson. Drake looked closely and saw Henderson now crying openly. Drake could not take it anymore.

Silently, end over end gaining speed as it neared its final destination, the throwing knife that left Drake's hand found its mark. Blood burst from Aurora's ribcage as the blade lacerated its way into her body, only stopping at the hilt. She shook once more, and the whimpering was over. Out of sympathy for Henderson, Drake had showed weakness. He killed the wolf.

Uncle would not be happy.

9 EVIDENCE

It sounded like a distant rolling thunder, only it was not thunder, and it certainly was not distant. The copper-jacketed lead rounds zipped through the woods tearing away at every leaf, stick, and tree trunk between the deputies and the twins as they ran down the hillside. The eerie sound made by the rifling slugs as they passed overhead was unmistakable. As if a whirling, zipping pocket of air was being ripped open directly above them, the boys continued their sprint through the foliage making their way to the river. The deputies did not follow in chase. The unknown steep terrain of the hill kept them in place on the game trail.

"Hold your fire! Hold your fire!" the sheriff demanded.

After the shots had stopped, they looked at each other in disbelief.

Boom! Boom!

Coleman's shotgun rang off another round from behind the rest of the group, startling them all. They all looked at him with disbelief. "What, I saw something move," he explained with his usual shit-eating grin.

"What the hell just happened?" Magee thought out loud, "And why did he only attack Aurora?" Upon hearing this, reality began to set in with the group. Someone had just killed one of their own. A deputy was dead.

"Gather some of these rocks and help me bury her," Ravizza said. He then added, "We say goodbye, then we go hunting."

Ravizza was not talking about hunting in the traditional sense, and the deputies knew it. This was no longer a manhunt. With the death of Aurora, it had become a mission of revenge. They gathered rocks and covered up the dog. Even doing so quickly, it took an hour's time to complete the task.

Picking up the last of the rocks that circled their fire pit, Henderson found the remainder of the arrow Tomek had shot. Pulling it from the coals, the stone head glowed red hot.

"What is that?" Coleman asked, seeing Henderson remove it from the pit.

She ignored him, knowing full well that the only reason he was looking at the fire pit was because she was bent over it.

"Sheriff, come look at this," Coleman proudly demanded as if he had found it himself.

"Who put that in there?" Magee asked.

"Probably Henderson!" Coleman answered quickly as she shot him a look.

"He put it there," the sheriff answered to break up the pending argument between his employees.

"Who, me? Not me ..." Magee pushed forward.

"Not you. Mowgli was here in our camp while we slept," the sheriff explained, pointing toward the barefoot tracks in the game trail. "We are not dealing with a normal kid. He has been out here for too long. He has learned to kill, and at this point, Mowgli is nothing more than an animal we must hunt."

The sheriff took the arrow and examined it closely, from the cedar-made shaft all the way to the now cooled-off head. He set the arrow down and began to remove his backpack and overcoat. The group just watched, circling around their boss with their eyes fixed on his every action. The sheriff reached down the front of his shirt, pulling out a loosely braided necklace. Attached at the end of the necklace was another arrowhead.

Holding them up to each other, the group could see that it was a direct match. Both heads were the same size, color, type of stone, cutting pattern, and weight.

"You see, me and Mowgli have a history, it seems."

"He made that necklace for you?" Coleman's question made the others roll their eyes in mockery.

"No, the arrowhead on my neck was not made for me, but it was meant for me. It came out of the shoulder blade of an elk. Not just any elk, though. It was embedded in the shoulder of the elk I hit when I put the cruiser into the laundry mat. I had wondered why that elk was sprinting through the middle of town, and I found the answer to that question when I opened him up to harvest what was still good of the meat. Someone had shot that bull just prior to my hitting him. Someone who used arrowheads exactly like this one."

Magee agreed that the heads were identical but remarked, "That was years ago. Mowgli would have just been a toddler."

"Yes, it was," the sheriff said again, examining the matching arrowheads. "Whoever shot that elk made both of these heads. Or they taught our Mowgli how to do it himself."

Walking over from his spot in the circle, Ravizza took the arrowhead from the sheriff and declared, "He killed your elk like he killed my dog. I now, too, will wear this head in a remembrance of our fallen Aurora until justice has been served."

Ravizza cut a piece of rope, tying a half-hitch knot around the head, and draped it around his neck. The sheriff and his crew had no idea how right his thoughts on the origins of the heads were. Uncle had indeed made both.

10 TWO BIRDS

With justice in mind, the group set course at daylight for the next point given to them on the GPS. They were headed directly for the orchard, and again would be within close distance to not only the twins themselves, but also their home.

Hours passed as they now hiked on trails that were nonexistent. Bushwhacking through thick brush and swamp land slowed their pace to not much more than a crawl. Not to mention they had been steadily climbing uphill through the day, putting them near the ridge of the valley. A summer sun and no breeze did not help with the mosquitoes and black flies who feasted on their hosts' bodies. Hot, tired, and angry, their defenses were down.

Even Ravizza and Henderson did not notice the tracks they walked upon. Paw prints went unnoticed as did the tufts of fur floating on the tops of the knee-high ferns. Step by step, slice by slice, as they cut their way through the brush, they got closer. Stopping for a break, Coleman leaned against a tree trunk. Sitting there drinking from his canteen, he raised his head, pouring the water over his face to cool down. When his canteen was empty, he brushed away the remaining splashes from his eyes only to realize what was above him. Their eyes met, and Coleman froze. Not being able to process exactly what it was, Coleman only could mutter a broken word.

"La, La ... La ... Lio ... n!"

Coleman was not given the time to finish the warning. The rest of the group had seen it just as he did, and although each of them was armed and could have easily shot at the attacker, they all instinctively fled in various directions. The traumatic events surrounding Aurora's death mixed with their weakened and somewhat lost states of mind made the group of deputies panic along with their leader. Each ran, crashing through the bush and swamps.

The cougar let out a shrieking roar as it soared down from its perch on the branch above. The big cat's fully extended claws dug deep into Coleman's shoulder as the impact took him to the ground. Fumbling for his shotgun, he rolled to his side as the cat sank its teeth deep into the thigh of the screaming deputy. Coleman quickly clutched the knife from his belt and thrust it into the left eye of the cat. The combination of the knife hitting bone and the blood on his hands made him lose his grip on the weapon as the cat whipped its head away from Coleman's leg. With all its power the cat was still much smaller than Coleman, who had now wrapped his other leg up and over the top of the cougar's back, scissoring the animal while he pulled its solid head to his chest in an attempt to break its neck. Interlocking his feet together, he rolled his body weight with all he had, spinning both him and the beast down a small drop off and onto a sandy ledge.

There, in the full sun, the man and cat slowly regained their balance and broke free of one another's grasp. Now both on their feet, they circled one another on the small landing. Both warriors were bleeding profusely from the wounds their respective challenger had inflicted, and yet neither were willing to die. Coleman glanced down to his left and saw bones. Looking to his right, there were more. Piles of bones.

"So, this is your pussycat graveyard, huh?" Coleman said to the cat as he realized he was now in the lair of the hunter. Claw marks on the nearby trees were evident from years of scratching and sharpening, as was the strong musky odor of the cat itself. It was the perfect spot for the cougar to lie, eat, and stalk prey. The ledge overlooked the entire valley, and it was clear to see that he had been watching the deputies' ascent all morning long.

Shotgun in hand, he knew the fight was over. Still, he waited to pull the trigger, admiring the predator that had chosen to take him on. Nearly showing the cat a modicum of respect, Coleman was going to let the animal run off, if it so chose. The cougar knew that Henderson would have been an easy kill, but the beast had chosen the largest of the group. The cat did not run, but continued to circle the deputy leering at him through the one uninjured eye as best it could. The cat lowered his back, digging his exposed front claws into the soft, sandy, fern-covered ground. As the tension built in his powerful hind quarters, both of them knew this was the moment.

Coleman quickly shouldered the gun just as the cat's front paws left the ground to spring toward him and pulled the trigger.

"Click."

The firing pin rang against the hammer inside the unloaded Remington 870. They say in these moments you can see your life flash before your eyes. Coleman did not see his life; he only saw one brief moment. The extra shots he rang off upon claiming to have seen something earlier in the day as the twins made their escape to the river had come back to haunt him. The degrading looks he received after firing off the two shots that were wasted, one of which was needed now more than ever, had distracted him from replacing the empty shells. Coleman knew in the brief second it took for the cougar to close the distance between the two of them in the air that he was going to die with an unloaded gun and a pocket full of ammunition.

Bracing himself on his ripped open leg, he waited for the impact of the cat's lunge. He closed his eyes and accepted his imminent fate. His only hope now was that the rest of the group would return to the scene and not allow his body to become part of the ominous bone pile.

However, the impact from the leaping cat did not come in the following seconds. The cat roared with the same fury of the previous attack, but Coleman felt no new pain. Only the throbbing sensation of blood flowing from his clawed shoulders and the gaping puncture wounds in his leg. Coleman opened his eyes to what sounded like a limb snapping. He watched a four-inch round ironwood tree flinging and flying upward through the air from the ground like a missile and into the canopy. The once-bent tree now stood straight up the way nature had originally intended. The cougar was then yanked onto its belly out its midair death pounce, slammed to the ground, and drug away off of the edge of the ledge. Swinging and fighting, pawing and clawing at the air as it now hung six feet off of the ground, Coleman dropped to his knees in shock. Thankful to be alive at the moment, the blood and dirt-soaked deputy did not care who had built the trap; all that mattered was they did and for that he was extremely grateful. Looking at the still-struggling cougar, he began loading shells into the magazine one by one.

Shhheeee click, shheeee click ...

Knowing full well that it would only take one shell to kill the hanging cat, he planned to use them all. The receiver and magazine were full after five rounds as he placed the butt of the gun stock on the ground. Utilizing the gun as a modified crutch, Coleman pulled his hulking body up to his feet. Bracing his weight on the gun, limping and dragging his mangled hamstring through the sandy fern-covered ground, he made his way slowly towards the still roaring cat. Shouldering the gun, he shot the cougar, killing it while it swung. Then again, again, and again. All five rounds found their mark, and he took a long, deep breath realizing he had escaped death and the battle was over.

Coleman knew damn well that cougars were not normally this far south, but they had taken a few complaints from farmers in the area losing livestock. He had to get a closer look and walked directly under the dead cat. While admiring the killing claws and fangs of the lifeless hanging cougar, his feet left the sandy soil and stepped onto a large patch of ferns. He felt his foot give way. Looking down, he knew it was not his injury that caused this. Unable to back up quickly with his injured leg, he fell forward into the fern pile.

The small twigs holding up the false fern floor snapped as the massive weight of the deputy broke through the top layer of the hidden pit trap. Tumbling uncontrollably into the pit, Coleman landed at the bottom of the eight-foot deep wooden spike-lined pit. Impaled, he looked at his chest to see a three-inch round wooden spike extruding through his navel.

Looking up with blood now coming out his mouth, he knew it was over. From the bottom of the dark pit, the hole above seemed so bright. Much like a train tunnel, his vision grew blurred and the tunnel began to close off, the light growing dim. Coleman focused his eyes once more to see the cat hanging there dead and the silhouettes of two faces leering over him from the top. He raised his hand to ask for help as his eyes struggled to see Tomek and Drake looking down on him. His arm dropped to the side as the last of his life faded away.

The twins had been in the trees the entire time watching the battle. Having again heard the group slashing through the brush, they were not hard to track. They had set both traps weeks ago in hopes of removing the problem cougar, but until today they were unsuccessful. Now not only was the cougar dead, but he took with him the biggest of the intruders.

Drake looked at his brother with a smile and said, "Two birds, one stone."

11 WAITING

The twins sat above the hole in the ground they had dug months ago, basking in the effectiveness of both of their traps' deployments.

"Where are the rest?"

"They ran like rabbits from a lion," Tomek answered his brother with a giggle. "How many are left?"

"There was five, plus the wolf."

"Four. We can handle four, no problem." Tomek's confidence had grown with each killing. "And one of them is a woman."

"A woman she might be, but there is something about her that is different than the rest. I am not sure about it, but she may be the most difficult for us to deal with."

Tomek scoffed at Drake's notion of taking out Henderson. Tomek had never dealt with women. Adding to the fact that he had never had a conversation with anyone outside of Uncle and Drake, there was no way he could know the power Henderson held over the two of them. With her interrogation skills and overall compassionate demeanor, the only way the twins would stand a chance was to eliminate her from afar.

"We will kill her for what she has done to us, just like the rest."

"What has she done, what have any of them done?" Drake asked, sensing the temper building in his brother. "I mean, the twin hunters killed our buck and they both tried to kill me, until you took out the first one and saved me." Floating Tomek's boat a little was enough to calm him down. Drake had been using this trick for years without Tomek becoming wise to it as taught to him by Uncle.

"Your brother is like the kettle on the fire. It is natural for him to steam, but once he boils the heat must be removed, or he will burn you."

"Yeah, I saved you all right, but you would have been fine."

"Either way, thanks, man."

"No worries."

Tomek often responded "No worries," but for the first time in their lives without Uncle, they had real worries.

"So, what's the plan?" Tomek referred to his brother when it came to the overall strategy they intended to use. He knew full well that Drake was the better brother for this situation. Tomek was also aware that complimenting his brother was equally appreciated.

"Take them out one by one, I guess; as long as they stay separated it shouldn't be too hard."

"Should we split up as well?"

"No, we must stay together. We are not as big, strong, or equipped as them."

"Blah, so they have guns. We are getting pretty good at dealing with these people who have guns," Tomek said, again ignoring the concern his brother was trying to impose upon him.

"Still, alone we are weak."

"Yeah, but we can take them out faster and get back to the

garden."

Drake found his brother's comment regarding the garden slightly hilarious based on the fact that the garden was the last place Tomek ever wanted to spend any amount of time.

"We are not splitting up. I need you. There, you happy?"

"Very," answered Tomek, but Drake knew the answer and was only asking facetiously. "I saw the woman head down through the brambles toward the river, and the dog guy went back toward their original camp."

Drake was happy that his brother could provide this useful intelligence, since he himself was watching the sheriff and Coleman's retreats. Drake bent down to pick up a stick and drew a rough outline of the area.

"Together they may have hunted us down, but apart they will all be scrambling back to Pine Run."

Tomek nodded in agreement.

"Their leader guy ran up toward the top of the ridge. He has a day and a half hike, but once he reaches the top, he may be able to call for help."

"So, we go after him first?"

Tomek always interrupted Drake's planning sessions like this. No matter what the topic, whether it was figuring out how to best plant corn, fix the roof, or kill intruders, Tomek did not have the patience to let the plan roll out in front of him.

"Not necessarily. Being the leader, he may try his best to recover his men," Drake pointed out.

"And woman," Tomek reminded Drake as if he forgot.

"Yes, Tomek. And woman."

"But that leaves one more. Where did he go?"

"Honestly, I have no idea," Drake replied, impressed that his brother remembered so much about their opposition. "They may have guns, but they are not woods people. You saw the way they camped. Add that to the fact that even though they dress alike, they do not operate as a team. I have a strong feeling they will show themselves to us in some way."

"Show themselves? What are you going wait for, them to run by us naked chased by a bear?" Tomek joked as he began to lose sight of the plan.

This time Drake spoke with confidence. "Night out here can be hard. We are used to it, and Uncle made us ready. They are not. If we don't get them, the woods will."

"So, what do we do now?"

"Wait. We wait them out."

"It is almost completely dark, so can we wait them out while trying to find the woman?" Tomek asked, again showing a peculiar interest in Henderson.

He did not like his brother's answer but agreed it was the better plan. "No, we know where she is. We need to find the lost one."

"Well, hopefully that bear chases him by us naked," Tomek added sarcastically.

"Why wouldn't the bear be naked?" Drake shot back quickly to show he could be just as quick-witted as his twin.

Not to be outdone, Tomek began to ask, "What if the bear was wearing the uniform of the lost guy …"

However, Tomek stopped mid-sentence looking over Drake's shoulder. Just as the loud conversations and bushwhacking of the deputies had alerted the twins to their location, the twin's own ongoing discussion had drawn unwanted and unexpected attention to themselves. Drake saw the look in his brother's eyes and spun to see what he was looking at. There stood Deputy Ravizza with his gun drawn a mere twelve feet away, demanding in an authoritative tone that the boys,

"Get on the ground! Get on the fucking ground now!"

12 PINE SLIDER

Ravizza stood behind them, pistol drawn nervously, moving back and forth between both boys. Time stood still for the deputy; all his training in both the Air Force and law enforcement never prepared him for this. The situation he was in now, with his gun drawn on two children, was never covered in his vast amount of training.

His mind raged full of mixed emotions. The rationalizing began with the fact that *"They killed Aurora, but could I really shoot a child."* Still, other thoughts raced through his mind straight to his trigger finger. Astonished that there were two of them, he continued to be unable to focus his aim on either of them.

"I am not going to tell you again. Get on the fucking ground!" Ravizza again demanded of the twins.

Frozen in place looking at his brother, Drake knew their only chance was to run. However, he could only hope that Tomek was thinking the same. Surveying the situation, Drake knew the bow slung over his shoulder was useless and reaching for a knife on his belt or ankle would surely get him shot. Seconds had gone by since they were first ordered to the ground, but in all three of their minds it felt as if hours had passed. Then, the silence broke.

"We both know you're not going to shoot me."

Ravizza was immediately taken aback by Tomek's boastful words.

"Stay there, back up, and get on the ground," the deputy ordered as Tomek slowly walked toward him with his hands up in a non-confrontational manner. Tomek, ignoring the stern request, continued walking slowly toward the now-retreating deputy.

Ravizza presented Tomek with one final warning. "One more step, son, and I am going to kill you."

Tomek responded with his own demands and a simple form of negotiation, which shocked Drake.

"No, you are not. You are going to let my brother go and then you can do anything you want with me. But if he is not allowed to leave, then one of us is going to kill you. Because we all know you cannot take us both down without killing us. And you, officer, are not a killer, are you?"

Looking Drake directly in the eyes, Tomek then asked, "Is that okay with you, Pine Slider?"

"Pine Slider? Why did he call me Pine Slider? Is it that he doesn't want them to know our names or is it ... ah, okay." Drake pondered until it dawned on him, and he knew Tomek's exact reasoning for calling him the wrong name. Drake looked at his twin again with a newfound appreciation for his tactile thinking and only nodded in agreement.

"Pine Slider? So that's your name?"

Drake nodded again, but this time it was in response to his enemy's questioning.

"Put your knives and anything else you have on the ground and leave, Pine Slider," Ravizza said while standing directly behind Tomek, using the boy's body as a shield. Having seen the thrown knife that buried itself into Aurora's chest make its impact, he was not taking any chances. He then turned his attention back to Tomek.

Drake did as he was told and slowly backed away from his brother and the deputy until he reached a short bend in the trail, which cleared him from their sight. Running as fast as he could directly to the top of the hill, he began surveying the valley as his new concern was getting ahead of the deputy who now had his twin brother in handcuffs walking swiftly toward the river. He knew that no one knew the wooded trails like he and Tomek and figured the deputy was headed toward the one thing that would lead them directly back to Pine Run – the river.

Getting ahead of them would not be the hardest part, knowing now that he was unarmed. He had to flank them, get ahead, and beat them to the pine rows adjacent to the river if he had any chance of stopping the well-armed deputy who had his brother in custody.

With the sun still high in the mid-day sky, Drake knew that even at a slow pace Ravizza and Tomek would reach the pines before the shadows in the valley grew. Drake would have preferred to deal with the situation in the dark. However, he was unaware of Ravizza's unique set of nighttime sky-reading skills. If the two of them were delayed at all, the sky would not be visible through the evergreen canopy in the pines.

Forty-plus years ago the logging industry had cleared out everything from the bottom land at the base of the hill ledges to the river on both sides. The region, being known for its dark hard-wooded walnut and oak forests, made it a magnet for the furniture and building industries. In order to turn the investment around as quickly as possible, the companies replaced the area with the much more quickly growing Northern White Pine that the rest of Michigan was famous for. The seedlings were planted in tight rows as far as the eye could see in an attempt to discourage branch growth. This provided tall, straight, knobless trunks. Within a few years, the pines resembled the rows of a library. Perfect man-made rows of tall trees with no branches and only green at the top.

Only these trees were never harvested again. The lumber yards did come back, but because of constant mechanical failures and equipment sabotage, they completely abandoned this section of the forest. Most of the workers, being Native American, held on to the overwhelming opinion that the land was cursed; Mother Nature was unhappy with how they had treated her. Removing the precious hardwoods and replacing them with pines grown in an unnatural way had so angered Mother Earth that she was the one causing all their problems, and only money would be lost in this land.

The twins knew that it was not Mother Earth who was the unhappy one. It was Uncle. Uncle had routinely shared with them his stories regaling the many months-long battle he had every night with the forestry crews. Never knowing a single man was the sole source of all their consternation, the lumber companies packed up and left to cut on the other side of Pine Run. Simply put, the companies no longer thought the pines were worth the trouble financially.

Sprinting through the underbrush in a downhill pattern, snaking his way through the brambles and thorns that tore at his exposed arms, Drake reached the edge of the library. The pines were a welcome sight as he entered them still at a runner's pace. His crashing effort alerted a flock of crows nesting in the thick evergreen tops and they erupted into flight, each displaying their displeasure at being interrupted with a cackling *"caw-caw-caw"* that could be heard through the entire valley as it echoed amongst the hills.

Smiling at the crows above him, Drake again felt Uncle's presence among them. Crows were not something they actively hunted and ate, but they were very useful. Knowing the language of the socially ganged-up birds meant you had a multiple sets of eyes above you.

"The long drawn out caaaaaaaawwww of a single crow is that of the sentry, the guard," Uncle would say. *"Caaaaaaaaw, caw-caw is the sentry letting his flock know there is something coming, or underneath them, but it does not present any danger. Look for deer or other wildlife moving in your area when you hear this.*

"The hunt is over when any crow in the flock meets you with a quick and short caw-caw-caw. This means danger and all the animals of the woods know it. All the animals will use the crows the same as you and I."

Working his way down one of the seemingly never-ending rows, Drake dropped to the side of his leg, sliding like a baseball all-star into a depression in the ground that the three of them had dug many years before. Multiple escape blinds like this existed throughout their trails in order to hide quickly if necessary. At the base of the dugout, a thick blanket of pine needles and branches sat atop an old burlap potato sack. The cover was propped up by a three-foot stick impaled into the ground. Not only was the spot located next to the main trail through the pines, but with the cover down, it was completely invisible. Both boys could fit inside each blind and appear as nothing more than a natural bump in the terrain. Drake had made it to the pine slider.

Planning to ambush the deputy as soon as they had unknowingly walked past him, he was extremely happy to not only be in the perfect spot, but that each blind contained a small supply box. Inside, Drake found matches, kindling, fishing line and, most importantly, a small hatchet.

13 HATCHET

"Those damn trash-eating birds never shut up, do they?" Ravizza said under his breath but loud enough for Tomek to hear. Tomek did not speak to him but only smiled to himself while looking at the ground, for he knew Drake was now in the pines and awaiting their arrival. Bumping the crows from their perch was no accident.

As the skies opened up to a cold, penetrating pouring rain that northern Michigan is known for, they continued working their way down the most obvious of trails. Tomek dragged his feet along the slushy sanded trail in an attempt to give his brother plenty of time to get set up in the pine slider. He was unable to wipe away the rain build up on his face due to the hard cold steel cuffs that kept his hands at bay as they dug into his wrists. This was a very uneasy feeling for Tomek. For the first time in his life, he was experiencing what it must feel like to be an animal caught in one of the many traps Uncle had taught them to set.

The only difference was Tomek knew he was not helpless. He knew they were getting close to the river, and the rain would wash away any tracks left by his brother ahead of them. Tomek knew that in just a few minutes he would be free of the shackles the uniformed beast had placed on him. He knew Drake was waiting in the pine slider, and his suspicions were confirmed as they turned the last bending corner through the hillside swale and entered the pines.

With the tops of the trees so thick and green, entering the pines was a welcome relief to both Tomek and Ravizza. The rain did not penetrate the pine floor, and it was as if they were under a dome. Moving along silently, it grew darker. Not only did the trees keep out the rain, but they effectively blocked out what light there was escaping from the storm clouds. In the darkness of the oncoming wet night, there it was. One-hundred yards ahead, the bump in the ground was visible only to Tomek as Ravizza followed him down the library row just to the left of it.

They continued down the path in the fading light, and as they grew closer, Drake could hear every step they made. Under the blanket of earth in the pine slider, he could not see them or know exactly where they were. He needed Tomek to give him some sort of a sign.

Tomek passed the pine slider, being careful not to look directly at it and tip off his trailing nemesis. As Ravizza stood directly in front of the pine slider, Tomek went to the ground on his knees.

"Get up," Ravizza demanded.

"I can't," Tomek said. "I'm tired, and we're almost to the river. You can hear it, can't you? Please don't make me try and cross the river. Please don't make me go into it at all."

Tomek was now pleading.

"I can't swim, and I watched my mother drown in that river. The river has caused everything that is terrible in my life." Tears began to mix in with the raindrops that collected on his head.

"Get off the fucking ground, or that's exactly where you're going," Ravizza said.

Tomek was putting on the show of a lifetime, and Drake enjoyed listening to it in some way. He knew his twin brother was simply telling the deputy these things to keep him in front of the pine slider. Drake was just waiting for the perfect moment to strike. Although Tomek's theatrical performance was straight out of one of the tales Uncle often told about a rabbit being thrown into a briar patch, Drake still was impressed with his brother's technique.

Tomek turned around, now facing Ravizza. Lifting his eyes to look him directly in the face, Ravizza could see the tears. He no longer saw a cold-blooded killer. In front of Ravizza was a broken-down, feral sixteen-year-old child who had nothing left in the world. Ravizza, a former orphan himself having bounced from foster home to foster home in his youth, now felt empathetic for the young man and the struggles he had been faced with.

"Please don't drown me like my mother. Just shoot me here. I should be dead anyway; I am an animal. Just kill me here, but please don't throw me into the river."

Watching and listening to this last round of dialogue, Drake rolled his eyes thinking that his brother was laying it on too thick. Having heard the briar rabbit story so many times, he hoped the deputy was not as familiar with it. Evidently, Ravizza did not pick up on the similarities in the stories because there, on the now-dark pine needle-coated forest floor, Ravizza holstered his weapon and placed out his arms, welcoming Tomek into his chest for an embrace.

Tomek stepped forward, halfway closing the distance while looking at Ravizza. The deputy extended his outstretched arms even further, gesturing what he now saw as a child forward. Tomek, looking into the eyes of Ravizza for assurance, took the last step and buried his sobbing face against the cold, wet, bullet-resistant vest that Ravizza adorned on the outside of his uniform.

Ravizza embraced the twin and patted him on the back. Tomek felt the deputy's right arm reach under his armpit and rest against him. As Ravizza closed his eyes and rested his cheek against the top of Tomek's head, he instantly flashed into shock as a tidal wave of pain surged up from his lower leg area.

When Ravizza's eyes closed and his head lowered, Drake had made his move. Rolling forward out of the pine slider, he swung and buried the hatchet deep into the back of the empathetic deputy's right ankle. As Ravizza dropped to the ground from his Achilles tendon being completely severed and hanging loosely, no longer connected, Tomek swung around the deputy's back and forced both of them to fall, slamming into the ground. In doing so, Tomek not only manipulated the deputy onto his own stomach, but the torque and pressure of the cuffs wrapped around Ravizza's arm caused his elbow to dislocate. If the popping sound at the moment of dislocation was not enough, the three of them knew his arm and gun hand were now useless as Ravizza lifted it up to see his forearm, wrist, and hand hanging loosely toward the ground as if it was only attached by the weak outer layer of skin.

Freeing himself from the tangled arm, Tomek stood to his feet. Still in shock from the pain of his injuries, the deputy lay on the ground rolling and muttering unintelligible words. The brothers looked at one another silently, smiling, contemplating what to do next.

Before the boys had a chance to decide, Ravizza came to and began reaching across his body with his uninjured arm in an attempt to cross-draw his weapon. The moment his hand made contact with the grip of the pistol, he could no longer feel it. Lifting his arm, the struggling deputy quickly realized why. His left hand was still on the pistol. However, his hand was no longer part of his arm. The hatchet Drake had thrown from three feet away removed it from his body in one fell swoop.

Bleeding profusely from both his ankle and his severed wrist, Ravizza attempted to scoot backward away from the twins. Digging into the ground floor with the heel of his boots, he tried to push himself back up the gentle slope of the path. His blood sat atop the brown fallen pine needles and glistened in the fading light. Looking at the boys, the deputy began to plead for their mercy.

"Please don't do this."

The twins slowly followed him as his blood stained the pine needle floor.

"First my dog, now me ..."

W.C. Hoffman

His attempts at both escaping and pleading became more labored as he continued to lose copious amounts of blood. Ravizza was not sure if he was seeing double from the pain or if somehow both twins were in front of him again.

"Think about what you are doing. Two wrongs do not make a right," the deputy said in his last attempt to be spared.

"What makes you think we are going to stop at two?" Drake replied while walking forward, picking up the hatchet. Still attached to the blade was the left hand with the pistol still in its grip. Drake removed the gun, handing it to his brother, full well knowing Tomek would love to add another firearm to his growing collection.

Tomek immediately pointed the gun at Ravizza and cocked the hammer back. Drake looked at his brother and quickly spoke up, "No sound."

As disappointed as Tomek was, he knew Drake was right in this instance. Drake then calmly stepped up to the shaking deputy who was now in shock from his wounds and blood loss. Rearing back and swinging forward with all his body weight, Drake implanted the hatchet directly into the top of Ravizza's skull where it remained lodged as the deputy's body lumped to the earth. Grabbing the handcuff keys off of the deputy's blood-soaked belt, he tossed them to his brother.

"Unlock yourself and help me drag his body into the pine slider," Drake said to Tomek.

Now free of the restraints, Tomek assisted his brother in dragging the body back to its final hiding place. They both scavenged the body,

97

removing any additional duty equipment that belonged to Ravizza.

"I, of course, get the gun, right?" Tomek asked, expecting a denial from his twin.

"Sure, but only until we get back to where you dropped your bow," Drake replied. Tomek felt it was a small victory and decided not to press the issue.

"Once they realize two of them are dead, they will know we are hunting them. We need to be as quiet and quick as possible," Drake continued.

"Now what?" Tomek asked in the pitch black of another Michigan night.

"One of these assholes will start a fire," Drake replied.

With that, they headed back up the hill to retrieve their weapons. Picking up his bow, Tomek lifted his nose to the air looking at Drake. Taking in a deep breath through his nostrils, he chuckled and shook his head.

"Smoke."

14 SMOKE

The fire was lit, still burning bright, as the twins laid eyes on it for the first time. Following their noses, they crested the hill and were both surprised to see the glow through the trees on the opposite side of the river. Neither brother had expected any of the invaders to cross the six-foot deep river. This time of the year hypothermia would not be a concern but the desire to be dry would explain the need for a fire.

"Do you think they swam?" Drake asked Tomek, knowing he was the one who spent the most time in the river trapping both muskrats and beaver during this time of the year.

"No, way too cold, but the only other way would be by boat," Tomek answered. As he uttered the word "boat," they both had the same thought. They thought of the birch tree dugout canoe they had hidden on the bank just up shore from their cabin. If someone had used their boat, they would have not only taken away the twins' chance to cross the river and chase them, but perhaps they had also found their home.

"Do we swim after him or go check on the dugout first?" Tomek asked.

"Is there a spot we can cross where it is shallower?" Drake again referred to his brother.

"Yeah, at the beaver damn that blocks off Shippen Run," Tomek said.

The Shippen Run was a spot where Uncle had built a small grinding stone press that used the current of the spring river to grind and mash both wheat and corn. The river's powerful ice floes, when melted, joined with the snow runoff in the hills each year, causing the river to rise above the dams and turn the wheel. The simple gearing Uncle devised from an old truck flywheel rotated the heavy circular grinding stone. This allowed them to process cornmeal and use the wheat they grew to make their own flour.

Drake knew the water there was only knee-deep thanks to the dams in the area, but he also knew that going that far upstream would mean not crossing the river until daybreak.

"We won't get there until light," Drake said.

"Yeah, I was thinking that as well. We should go check on the dugout canoe," Tomek said.

"Wait. There is one more way to cross without getting wet," Tomek added.

"Okay?" Drake questioned with a lowered tone that mimicked the way Uncle often spoke.

"The tree legs!" Tomek proudly bolstered, referring to a set of seven-foot tall stilts they often used in the orchard to pick fruit from the tops of the apple trees.

"You are a freaking genius," Drake said while smiling in amazement at his brother's increasing cleverness.

Tomek was thankful of his brother's praise, but it wasn't his idea. Uncle and Tomek had used the stilts to play in the river a few times in the past when Drake was off doing other activities. Uncle would stand in the summertime water and let Tomek don the stilts. This made the boy much taller than Uncle for the water-bound wrestling match that was about to take place between the two of them. Uncle would laugh wholeheartedly as Tomek failed to keep his balance while wrestling and continually splashed down into the river.

It wasn't something they were hiding from Drake, but it was kind of their own thing that they enjoyed together. Needless to say, it still wasn't something Tomek was going to share with his brother; he was more than fine letting Drake think it was all his own idea.

With the cabin a forty-minute hike back upriver, and the orchard on the way, the plan was set. They made the hike and kept out of sight on the river's edge; staying just inside the tree line allowed them to keep a constant eye on the glowing fire. Knowing their next target's camp was across the river up on the facing hillside, they worked quickly once inside the orchard, gathering up the stilts and the worn leather lashes that were used to attach them to their legs. The time spent inside the orchard would be the only time the twins would take their eyes off of the fire, and both were relived as they again reached the river to see it still burning bright.

With only one set of stilts, Tomek was first to cross and did so with ease. Each step was made calmly and confidently. His years of experience showed, as operating the stilts on the loose rock floor of the river against the moving current was not an easy task. Once across the river, he banded the stilts together with a piece of rope. The opposite end was tied to an arrow shaft which he shot over the water's edge back to Drake waiting on the other side.

Drake pulled the rope, dragging the stilts back to the shoreline and then placed them on his legs while sitting atop of a large rock. Once standing, Drake took his first step and immediately knew this was not going to be easy. He also felt a little embarrassed at the skill his twin had shown just minutes before, yet he knew other than swimming, this was going to be the only way.

Drake's legs wobbled, and he bobbed back and forth with each step. Tomek could not help but laugh at his brother's struggles.

"Keep waving your arms like that and maybe you will fly over!" Tomek yelled, but he was glad to see Drake finally making some progress.

At the halfway point, Drake began to move along much more quickly and realized that staying angled into the current provided a bit of a balancing fulcrum that stabilized the stilts.

Tomek turned around to look downriver and up the hillside to check on the fire when he heard the splash. Turning back to face the river, he could not help but laugh. Drake was again flailing his arms around, but this time in an attempt to swim through the fast flowing river.

"What happened?" Tomek asked as Drake reached the shore, pulling his body up arm over arm in an army crawl fashion as his legs, still attached to the stilts, made them useless as a swimming aide.

"I fell."

Drake's answer was simple enough and all that was needed.

"You didn't have to do that; it is not even close to Memorial Day," Tomek said, now openly making fun of his brother.

Tomek was referring to an old tradition the boys had with Uncle. Uncle, being a man of the military, still held on to and passed along some of the societal holidays and traditions. Especially those holidays that pertained to the armed forces. The boys knew that many men and women had died for the country, and while they had no reverence toward any country or nation, they did have respect for the fallen soldiers.

Uncle would say *"I knowingly sent them to die. Those were the orders I was given and for that, one day a year sure as hell is not enough."*

Thus, every year on Memorial Day, the boys and Uncle would do no work. They would enjoy a peaceful day usually fishing for the spawning pan fish that would be on their beds. No matter if the fishing was good or not, a large meal was enjoyed along with a moment of silence and reverence around their fire that night.

Memorial Day always marked the first swim of the spring as well, and the three of them would jump in the icy cold river. This was the tradition that Tomek was referring to while poking fun at his cold brother. Even in the hot years, they would get in and then immediately jump out as the water was known to take your breath away and send instant shivers. The ice-cold swim, Uncle said, would *"Clean your soul of the winter grime trapped inside."*

Winter grime or not, Drake was not enjoying this plunge into the river as he would his yearly jump into the same waterway. Unlatching the stilts from his legs, his body fell into an instant numbness. There in the dark along the rocky bank, Drake started to remove his wet clothes as best he could. Tomek assisted, and Drake was quickly naked and still shivering. The cold night air not only steamed his hot breath as it left his body, it also chilled him further as it entered his lungs. Tomek ran back to where he had placed his bag and retrieved the bloodstained coat along with the other duty gear they had removed from Ravizza a bit ago.

Drake quickly threw it on, zipping it up and pulling it close to his body. Holding his left arm up, Drake smirked as an eight-inch chunk of the coat's arm was missing from his hatchet throw.

Tomek seeing his brother's blues lips force out the smile said, "You ruined a nice coat, dumbass."

Too cold and still shivering, standing on the shore line naked from the waist down, Drake looked at his brother and said, "Happy Memorial Day, Uncle."

"He would have loved to see that fall," Tomek said.

"I am pretty sure it was his spirit that pushed me!" Both brothers laughed quietly as they worked together on ringing out the water from Drakes pants and underwear.

"Swim back across, go into the cabin, and warm up again. I'll take out the fire starter," Tomek suggested.

"Not going to happen. Not only am I not getting back in the water, I am not going to send you off alone while I sit inside," Drake said, shooting down the preposterous idea. "Let's go climb the hill, find the fire, do what we got to do with whomever started it, and enjoy the warmth of it."

Drake's plan sounded fine to Tomek, and he knew all along that would be the outcome.

Slipping his pants and boots back on, Drake led Tomek up the hillside to the west of where they had known the fire to be, figuring it was built on the old logging tram road that was the only flat part of the entire ridge almost all the way into Pine Run. The six-foot-wide tram road would provide the fire starter with both a nice spot to camp, as well as protection from the chilling winds that kicked through the valley.

Walking west and coming in from directly above the fire would give them a tactical advantage. It might take an hour longer to reach the fire, yet at this point they were hoping to catch the starter asleep or at least in a state of physical weakness due to his or her unpreparedness.

Once above the still-glowing fire, the twins looked down upon it from over 100 yards away. From this distance and height, they could make out the camp very well in the flickering light of the small, dwindling fire. Being this close meant the brothers did not speak, yet neither of them needed to. This type of hunt had been played out so many times in their past that they both knew exactly what the other was going to do. Granted, this was always on the bedded deer that rested on the same tram roads, but in the recent past they had become

incredibly adept at hunting and killing the humans that use them as
well.

Tomek worked his way down toward the camp, staying above it on
the boulder outcroppings that jutted out from the hill. Stalking on top of
the moss-covered, glacier-placed rock tops allowed him to be silent and
get close without waking the subject, who he could now clearly see was
lying in a sleeping bag tucked under the rock ledge much like the ones
he used to obtain his new position thirty-five yards away. Frustrated
with his position because he had no clear bow shot into the sleeping
bag that would end it now, he stuck with the plan and watched as Drake
worked his way down to the campsite using the same rocks in the
opposite direction.

Dropping onto the tram ground as silent as an owl in flight, Drake
held his tactical knife in one hand and his newfound favorite weapon,
the hatchet, in his other. At twenty yards he was still in the dark, and
while Drake could not fully see him, he knew something was there in
the shadows. Continuing forward, digging the heels of his still wet boots
into the ground first followed by a gentle footfall at every step in order
to stay silent, he approached the sleeping soon-to-be victim.

At ten yards, Drake was just outside the camp and was in full fire-
light view of his brother. Drake was in throwing distance of the bagged
fire starter but wanted to close the distance just a few more feet to
confirm a proper target. He made three more steps, then flipping the
knife around in his hand so that the well-balanced blade was in his
fingertips, Drake reared back to throw the knife, stretching for power

with his arm extended behind him.

Booooom!

Drake never heard the rifle shot from Magee's sniper rifle but felt the direct impact as the 30.06 round struck his chest. Tomek watched in horror as the force of the bullet's penetrating impact violently threw his brother to the earth and off of the tram road where he knew it was at least an eighteen-foot-drop. Still, Tomek stayed silent, realizing for the first time in a while he was afraid—afraid and angry.

15 Alone

Tomek was angry they had fallen for the trap, angry that there never was anyone in the sleeping bag to begin with. Tomek was angry at the fact that someone had just shot and killed his twin brother, from a distance, with a gun, like a coward. His desire to run to his brother's body was quelled by the fact that the body was now the bait. Tomek knew where the shot came from and knew the killer would soon be back to either check out his kill or pick up his camp.

Now it was a waiting game—waiting to kill. There would be time to burn his brother and put his ashes to rest with Uncle tomorrow. The feeling of losing his brother to a gunshot made him finally understand Uncle's views on firearms. There is no skill, no pride, and no reverence in that type of death.

"Drake deserved better," he thought to himself. After two silent hours the fire was completely out, and darkness had reclaimed its grasp on the hillside. Growing more and more impatient, Tomek was thrilled to see the light. Light was emanating not from the moon, the stars, or even the dawn, but a piecing light shining down the tram road.

The shooter had turned on his flashlight and come to claim his trophy. Tomek waited, hand on the bow string, fingers surrounding the knock as he continually repeated to himself *"In the name of my brother,*

I will kill you."

Both Tomek and Magee moved toward the camp. Magee shuffled along through the fallen leaves with much less caution than that of the predator on the rocks above him. Now only twelve feet away, Magee was still very unaware that he was not alone. Tomek, with his bow drawn and hand at its anchor point just under his cheek bone, stood there wanting to kill the deputy. Only he felt that simply killing the shooter of his brother with an arrow from behind was not enough.

"This demon must pay for what he has done."

Again, the anger was boiling inside of Tomek.

Reaching the edge where Drake's body had rolled off into the valley, the deputy illuminated the area with his flashlight. There, just below the edge, was the body of what he knew to be Mowgli. The murdering boy that, as far as he knew, had taken out two hunters and a police K-9 unit. Drake did not look so menacing now in the dim light's beam. The boy lay there on his side with his arm draped over his head, face down in the dirt with the remains of frothy blood still surrounding his mouth.

The flashlight hitting his brother's body also allowed Tomek to see his dead twin for the first time. Deciding it was time to begin his mental assault, he picked up a stone and tossed it into the roots of a tree just ten feet from Magee.

Magee jumped to the side as the stone plinked against the tree. Drawing his pistol and holding his light across the top of his gun arm in a tactical fashion, he quickly realized nothing was there but a tree. As fast as Magee had confirmed he was alone, a barred owl called from his perch behind him.

"Who-who-who, whoooo ..."

The startled deputy spun 180 degrees, now illuminating the tree line where the owl had previously been roosted. The beam's subtle shake, coupled with the deputy's labored breathing, allowed Tomek to see that his brother's killer was slowly losing his nerve here in the dark woods, thanks both to Tomek and the random bird of prey.

"Who-who-who, whoooo," the owl cried out, this time from just over Drake's body, again causing Magee to spin in fear while pointing both his light and the gun at the noise coming from what seemed to be every direction.

For Tomek, the barred owl was a welcomed guest to this kill party. Uncle's teachings on stealth and camouflage often relied upon the skills owls displayed in the wild. Both boys could identify every owl species by its particular call, often translating them into English. The barred owl now terrorizing Magee was no different.

"Who, who cooks, who cooks for you?" the call of the barred owl rang out again from a different spot. Again, Magee spun in an attempt to discern the source of the sound. Only this time, the owl was directly above Tomek's head. As the light beam hit Tomek in the face, his fingers released the bow string.

Magee, astonished at what his flashlight had shown him, had no time to acquire the target and shoot. Magee never saw the arrow in flight, and as the razor-sharp stone head made contact with the glass lens of the flashlight, it shattered, breaking the bulb and forcing both the light and his gun to flip out of his hand to the ground. The arrow had also ricocheted off of the light and toward Magee's mouth, knocking out multiple teeth on impact and slicing the right corner of his face. The arrow left a gash in his cheek from mouth to ear.

Now Magee found himself in total darkness, bleeding profusely. While attempting to not choke on the warm iron-like blood that began pouring into his throat, he dropped to the ground in a frantic search for the pistol that had, unbeknownst to him, fallen off the ledge behind him. Tomek leapt down from his perch on to the rock and, even through the dark, he could see Magee on the ground searching for his weapon.

"Who are you?" Magee yelled upon hearing Tomek land. The words were strained coming from his torn-open mouth while he spit out gobs of coagulated blood mixed with broken tooth fragments.

"I am the night, I am the fire, I am the owl, and I am the woods," Tomek answered while circling Magee, who was still on his hands and knees looking into the darkness asking,

"What do you want?"

"How are you alive?"

"I fucking shot you."

Tomek, realizing that Magee had not yet put together that there was more than one of them, decided to continue answering the deputy in a terrorizing manner with a deeper, almost growling voice.

"You cannot kill what is not alive."

Tomek then drew back his bow and aimed for the small spot

between the eyes of the deputy and was instantly blinded by a flash of light.

The sound of the gunshot echoed through the valley. Every owl and crow in the area called out as they took flight from their roosts. Tomek never had the chance to release the arrow as the muzzle flash from the gunshot caused him to flinch off his target. The instant brightness of the flame escaping out the end of the barrel was gone as quickly as it had arrived.

Both Tomek and the deputy looked each other directly in the eyes through the darkness using what little moon had peaked through the cloudy sky. Tomek dropped his bow, feeling around his entire body, searching for where the round had struck him. Looking toward the deputy again, he made eye contact as Magee slowly fell forward from his knees, hitting the ground with a thud that launched leaves into the air upon impact.

The clouds dissipated just enough for Tomek to look fifteen yards up the tram road. Again, he was locked eye to eye with a shooter, frozen, as if believing if he did not move, the shooter would not be able to make him out in the dark. Motionless, hidden in the shadows, he watched as the new shooter walked slowly up to Magee's body.

Picking up his bow and raising it slowly with the same arrow knocked that was meant to kill Magee, Tomek came to full draw, waiting for his new target to take one more step into the beam of moonlight.

Just prior to reaching the light, the shooter stopped, looked into the dark area where Tomek stood to the side of the boulder and hollered, "You cannot kill what is not alive."

Tomek did not understand how or why, but hearing Drake's voice in the dark was nothing short of miraculous.

16 Wounds

Stepping out from his shadowed hiding spot behind the boulder, Tomek grasped Drake in his arms, pulling him close, chest-to-chest in a deep hug that caused Drake pain.

"Ah, aaaah, ouch, careful," Drake said.

"How the hell, I saw you get shot!" Tomek said, still holding tight to his back-from-the-dead brother.

"I guess when I put the coat on it had some sort of a lining in it that stops guns," Drake said, referring to Ravizza' bullet resistant vest-lined coat that had just saved his life.

"Are you hurt at all?"

"Yeah, the bullet didn't break my skin but I am pretty sure it broke my rib cage or something. It hurt like hell once I woke up."

"Woke up?" Tomek asked, puzzled.

"Yeah, the impact knocked me out, I guess. How did I end up down there?"

"You fell."

Drake rolled his eyes at his brother's obvious answer but did not want to push the conversation.

"What woke you up?" Tomek inquired.

Drake didn't say anything. He just smirked and held up the pistol that Tomek's arrow had forced out of Magee's hand and over the edge of the tram road.

"Well, I am glad you woke up, even though I didn't need you. I had him dead to rights anyway," Tomek said in his usual boastful manner.

"You needed me as bait, and I drew him out for you," Drake said, taking off the jacket and looking at his chest for the first time. "Too dark here to see much, but it's already bruised. Let's head back to the cabin so I can wrap my chest."

"Sounds like a good plan to me. I'm hungry anyway."

Tomek led the way back down the hillside using the easiest route that could be carved out in the dark. The topic of their conversation was light-hearted. Both seemed happy to be not only alive but together.

"What is going to happen when if we don't get them all?" Tomek asked.

"Well, I'm sure they will come back with more. But just like Uncle with the lumber company, if we keep making it hard for them each time, hopefully they will eventually just quit."

Tomek was satisfied with his brother's answer, but they both knew it was the simple way out. Their lives had been forever changed, and this valley was no longer only theirs.

"What about the bodies?" Tomek asked.

"I thought about that earlier. We will have to collect them for burning later. If we light a fire big enough to break bones, when we're done, it will for sure give away our position," Drake said.

"Or we use the fire as a trap," Tomek said.

"It would work at least for one of them, but I'm hurt. You would be alone. If they came together, we could be in trouble," Drake said.

"How long will you need to rest?" Tomek asked as they reached the river.

"There will be time to burn them and break bones later," Drake said, reluctant to admit he had no clue just how injured he truly was. "Just stay focused. We need to eliminate them all first."

"How long will you need to rest?" Tomek asked again, this time hoping for a valid answer.

"I have no idea, but there is no way I can pull a bow back," Drake said.

"Good thing you have a gun now, then, huh?" Tomek teased.

"Hahaha, ouch, ouch … don't make me laugh," Drake said, as his laughter was met with severe pain in his ribcage.

"Are you ready to go swimming again, brother?" Tomek asked, picking up the stilts. "With your injury, there is no way you will be able to use these."

"Walk your ass across the river, go get the dugout, and come get me." Drake was not asking, he was demanding.

"Walking all the way upriver to get the canoe and then coming back down in the dark to find you, not to mention we will still be downriver of home and will have to walk back up …" Tomek's negative tone was interrupted by Drake.

"Fine, I will wade back across. We are going home anyway, so I can warm up again there."

Tomek sat atop a fallen tree that branched out into the river and put the stilts on. He began to cross the river again with ease, showing off his balancing skills, this time in the dark. Annoyed, Drake stepped into the water at the edge and stood there, knee-deep and building up the courage to wade in farther.

As he leapt forward again, the ice cold rushing flow of the water stole his breath and forced him to cough, which in return made his ribcage feel as if it were on fire. Only this time was not as bad as the first, he thought. The frigid cold of the river also felt good on the outside of his injured body. The cold bullet vest-lined jacket remained pressed to his ribs, providing some pain relief, and it helped control some of the swelling. Jumping forward with his legs under the water and letting the current take him a bit downstream until his feet landed again seemed to be the easiest way to move, as both arms were useless for traditional paddling. Keeping his left arm at his side, pressing the coats interior against his chest, he made his way even with his stilted brother.

Slowly inching his way closer and closer, Drake was silent as he finally reached his brother at the halfway point of the river. Knowing they were headed back to the cabin was reason enough for Drake to kick out the left stilted leg of his twin and watch Tomek plummet from his perch, joining him in the river. The splash alone was enjoyment enough, as Tomek's flailing arms and legs did not make for a graceful entrance into the water.

Tomek's head was back above the surface as quickly as it had gone under. Swimming arm over arm, dragging the stilts still connected to his legs behind him, he struggled until reaching the shore line. Joining him at the shore, Drake held his breath in an attempt to keep from laughing and inflicting further pain upon his now-numbing chest.

Drake enjoyed watching Tomek squirm about trying to unhook his legs from the stilts. Untying the knots was no easy task with bitterly cold, wrinkled fingers. As Tomek sat there, he looked up to see Drake standing above him with a large smile.

"Ha ha ha, jerk," Tomek sneered.

Drake remained silent, shivering as he too was cold from the swim, but for some reason this time being soaked was not as harsh as his first fall into the river. Drake held tight looking down at his brother with delight. Given his ribs were not throbbing at the moment, he forgot about the challenges he and his brother still faced.

"Aren't you going to say something?" Tomek asked, beginning to think his brother's stare was bordering on creepy.

Drake smiled, turned to walk away, and said, "Happy Memorial Day."

17 Sun Rise

Opening the hollowed-out oak tree door to the cabin was a welcome sight for both of the twins. Having restlessly battled for almost forty consecutive hours, the brothers were cold, wet, hungry, and hurting. Entering their home again instantly made them forget the two remaining troubles who awaited them in the woods.

There was something about the smell in the hill residence. It could have been from the birch bark and alabaster that lined the walls and ceiling for years, or just the fact that there was little to no airflow. The cool dryness of the stale-smelling home was so ingrained in their heads that even the slightest whiff of something similar out in the wild would make them think of home.

The twins were quick to strip themselves of their wet clothes and find clean, dry replacements from their stash of surplus camouflage fatigues. While the fire in the wood stove had gone out shortly after they originally left the cabin days before, the ground was well-insulated and it had not been anywhere near freezing outside. The semi-warm cabin was a pleasant and welcomed comfort.

Tomek sat on his bed fumbling with Magee's handgun, which he had taken out of his brother's soaked backpack as quick as Drake set it down. Removing the magazine and each of its rounds, he meticulously dried each one of them by hand, polishing the brass to make them appear brand new.

"What is your fascination with the guns, man?" Drake asked.

"Well, it seems to me they have been a big help. I mean, if not for this gun right here, we might both be dead," Tomek reasoned, proud to prove his point.

"If not for gunshots going off, we would not be able to track these people either," Drake reminded him while quietly sitting in pain watching his brother complete the cleaning and reloading of the pistol. "What now?"

"I am going to keep it right here just so we both know where it's at," Tomek said, walking by Drake and laying the pistol down in a cubby about the size of a small bucket they had dug out of the side rock wall years before.

"Why there?" Drake asked, knowing there was no better hiding place inside the cabin but wanting to see if the two of them were again on the same page without discussing it. Tomek ignored the question, only looked at the cubby and worked out the perfect placement.

"Be gentle when you set it down there," Drake warned his brother.

"Why?" asked Tomek sarcastically. "It's not going to go off. Quit worrying."

"You know damn well why you'd better be gentle. That's the entire reason you are using that particular cubby, isn't it?" Drake asked, knowing his brother could not ignore that comment.

"Yep, great place for a gun, huh?" Tomek replied, smirking.

Drake knew the cubby was probably the perfect place for a weapon and was a little annoyed with the fact that Tomek had come up with using it. In an attempt to prevent his twin's ego from overinflating, Drake just rolled his eyes and offered a resigned, "Yep."

Drake then headed over to the hand-built hickory medicine cabinet to look for what was left, if anything, of Uncle's old medicine supply. Disappointed to only find a large supply of penicillin, he turned around to talk to Tomek.

"Grab me a beeswax candle from …" Drake stopped his sentence short in the observance of his twin brother already fast asleep in the cot.

"Never mind. I'll get it myself," he thought.

Reaching above the cots to the cupboard that held the candles was painful, but the stretch did have a therapeutic feel to it. Bumping his leg into Tomek's cot caused his sleeping twin to roll over and mumble something about "killing the girl."

Drake rolled his eyes and felt somewhat sorry for his brother who seemingly could not even rest in his sleep without dreaming about their next fight.

Lighting the candle, Drake was able to see for the first time the extent of the damage done to his ribs. Magee had shot him just above his left nipple. Without the tactical Kevlar coat of Ravizza, the lead round would have disintegrated Drake's heart, causing an instant death.

While instant death was certainly not the outcome, a large dinner plate-sized blue and purple contusion was. Feeling around with his fingers, he could not confirm any actual broken bones. Drake began to think he may have escaped the entire ordeal with just muscle and tissue damage. He knew that without some sort of medical intervention, the muscles in and around his wounded area would tighten up, rendering him useless in the remaining fights against Henderson and the sheriff.

"*Healing oils. I need to make Uncle's healing oils,*" he thought to himself as he began rounding up the supplies located throughout the cabin. This task in itself was not an easy one. Moving around basically underground in the dark of the glowing candle to collect items strewn about with an intense pain was almost more than he could handle.

Having collected what he believed to be everything he needed, Drake sat down at the main table they used for making weapons and eating meals during the cold months. Drake lit another beeswax candle he and Uncle had made from last year's abundant supply that was gathered from their colony of hives kept in the orchard. Each handmade candle was four inches around and three inches tall and would provide several hours of both heat and light. Right now, it was the heat that interested Drake.

Placing the candle inside of a baking pan they used for roasting meals, he lit the handmade braided willow wick. The light of the second candle, now burning on the small table, was enough to cause Tomek to roll back over and face the wall while grumbling about the girl again in his sleep.

Drake then placed a small six-inch terracotta flower pot they had used to grow a tomato plant the previous summer upside-down over the top of the candle with the rim resting on top of pan sides, allowing air to flow through the pan and up under the pot. Placing a Petoskey stone on top of the small hole in the pot kept the flame's heat inside, causing it to quickly heat up the exterior of the pot itself.

Grabbing a larger terracotta pot, Drake again placed it upside-down over the smaller pot with the rim also resting on the sides of the pan. Leaving the small one-inch hole on the bottom of the larger pot uncovered forced an abundance of hot air inside the pots to exit through it. The hot air that aggressively escaped through the second pot's hole was replaced by air being drawn in from the bottom and rushing to feed the flame. This caused the unit to produce a soft but constant roaring "hiss" upon reaching the perfect internal temperature.

The simple homemade convection torch was, of course, taught to them by Uncle for times when they needed to centralize a direct heat source. The air escaping the top hole could quickly turn a metal rod red hot. Uncle used this method any time he may have needed to melt lead to fix a tool or for heating steel while forging knives.

With the terracotta pot convection oven now putting out heat at full capacity, Drake enjoyed the extra warmth it added to the room as he began separating fresh wintergreen leaves he had stored in a jar from their stems. Placing the small pieces into a bowl as he ripped them up, Drake savored the fragrance they emitted. However, it was not the fragrance he was after.

Uncle and the boys had spent many hours walking in the woods collecting anything they were to find that may be useful along the way. Wintergreen was one of their most sought-after items. Chewing on the tasty leaves alone was a pleasure, but their real magic was held inside the leafy stems themselves. Grinding and boiling the leaves released menthol. Menthol was very useful to them for many skin ailments, including rashes and the occasional simple sunburn. Upon coming into contact with the skin, the menthol would open the pores, providing an almost instant cooling sensation.

The final ingredient to Uncle's healing oil was as simple and abundant as could be in their northern Michigan home. Rotten birch bark was not only littered across every acre of their valley, but it also lined the walls of their cabin.

The key to using the birch was to find a dry piece that had decomposed to the point where its physical structure was breaking down, causing the inside layers to become stringy and hair-like. The decomposing process stripped the bark of its protective layers and sugars, allowing the bark to release its natural anti-inflammatory properties.

Not wanting to pull a piece of back from the wall, Drake quickly, quietly, and cautiously stepped outside the front door. Moving the oak tree door was more of a chore with his sore chest than he had imagined it would be, but he managed to do and returned with an old piece of bark from a nearby blow-over without waking up his brother.

Drake placed a glass soda bottle they had found years before on top of the terracotta pot's hole. The bottle was about half full of water and would quickly come to a boil, at which point he would place the string-like strips of birch into the bottle. Boiling them took a few minutes longer than the wintergreen, giving Drake a chance to go run their small kitchen hose out to the river. With the hose placed underwater and held there with a small rock, Drake returned inside where the other end of the hose came up from its buried position in the floor into the small sink.

Drake began hand-pumping the air out of the hose with an improvised vacuum made from an old hot water pad that Uncle had stuffed with a large sponge. Squeezing the bag over and over for about three minutes was all that was needed to have a steady constant supply of siphoned river water into their sink. With the cold water flowing in from the river, positioned in the sink was an old, rusted red tin coffee can. The can itself was not important, but it held inside of it a coil of copper piping about a quarter of an inch in diameter. One side of the pipe contained a funnel, and the other was an open spout with a cap on it extruding out from the bottom of the can. Drake placed the hose in the can, and it filled up quickly with the cold running water from the river. Leaking out of the rusted holes in the coffee can and out of the top allowed the river to continually provide the condensing coil with chilled, flowing water.

Seeing that the bark strand had softened up and sloped down into the bottom of the glass bottle, he knew it was time to add the wintergreen. In doing so, Drake was making sure to get every last leaflet and sprig in the bottle. Now, he had to wait. He placed the funnel over the glass bottle and watched as the vapors produced from the boiled down ingredients nature had provided entered the funnel and came to rest inside the cooling coils.

Once inside the coils, the menthol, water, and anti-inflammatory vapors would distill back into a liquid that had oil-like consistency. Drake watched closely, confirming he had good water flow through the tin can throughout the distillation process, which was required in order to properly cool down the vapors inside the coil.

The coil began to make a popping noise and thump around inside the tin can. This allowed Drake to know that the coil was filling and would be ready to open soon. Pulling the cork stopper from the end of the tube allowed the oil to flow out into the bowl Drake had ready. Filling the bowl rather quickly, Drake set it aside and began cupping his hands directly under the spout. As they filled, he splashed the cool oil onto his bruised chest.

As the menthol opened up his pores, the cool burning sensation was a welcome relief. With his pores open, the birch was allowed to work its magic and enter the affected areas. As quick as the coil had begun flowing, it was soon empty again. Drake removed the funnel and bottle from the oven.

Deciding to leave the oven going to heat the room, Drake tilted the other beeswax candles' melted wax into the bowl of healing oil. Combining the oil and the wax made a cream-like substance that could be rubbed on and into the skin, allowing hours of relief compared with the seconds that the oil alone provided. It also made the homemade medicine spill-proof, as well as providing it with a much longer shelf life.

Stirring the cream and applying it to his bruised body, Drake felt the cooling action and a sense of pride. This was the first time he had made it alone without Uncle's guidance. Lying there in his bunk, Drake finally rested and closed his eyes, quickly drifting off to sleep only waking periodically to adjust his position as none of them allowed him total comfort with the soreness in his chest.

With each awakening, Drake would reapply a healthy coat of healing balm. As the sun began to rise, he was pleased to find that, for the first time in hours, he could take deep breaths with little to no pain.

Getting up with the sun, opening the door, and watching the sunrise crest the mountains, Drake remembered what he loved the most about their way of life here in the woods. It was something maybe Uncle had forgotten over his years of pain.

It was the fact that in the woods, they were always alone yet always together.

18 River Bend

Drake's moment of enjoying the peaceful morning sunrise quickly changed as he glanced upriver. Slowly meandering its way, floating toward him, bobbing up and down in the gentle rapids without someone paddling it, was their dugout canoe. Not wanting to lose the boat, he pondered his options. Drake was not looking forward to entering the river yet again to swim out and snag it before it passed by, but he knew without some luck that would most likely be his only choice. Or, perhaps, the river might help him out. He began running downriver to cut it off at the bend, hoping it would wash up on the river's sharp turn.

Running as fast as his injured lungs allowed him to breathe, he gained altitude on the hillside to avoid having to climb over the large rocks on the side of the riverbank. The cold morning air in his lungs felt good against the pain of his sore muscles. Exhaling out the cold morning air and watching it become instant mist was equally painful. However, any pain and concern about his lungs was quickly set aside in his mind as the canoe continued to make its way toward him.

Looking down from his hillside perch, the boat, which was almost parallel with him on the river, gave Drake enough height clearance to see what had set the boat free from its moorings where they stored it upriver at Shipen Run. Down in the cavity of the floating dugout was Deputy Henderson. Cold, shivering, and balled up in the fetal position, she did not have the strength to paddle the vessel and was relying on the river to save her.

Just as Drake hoped, the boat came to rest on the shoreline at the river's bend. Drake had watched every large stump and log that took the same path end up there over the years, so the canoe doing the same was not a guarantee but also no surprise.

Standing there a mere five yards away from the beached vessel, Drake reached for the throwing knife kept on his hip only to realize that he began chasing down what he thought was an empty boat without gathering a single piece of weaponry or gear. Watching the boat while pondering what to do, Drake knew his chest was too injured to risk a hand-to-hand fight, even if it was against a woman.

His eyes remained fixed as there were no signs of movement. He knew at this point the woman was either already dead or incredibly weak.

"I should sneak back and get Tomek, or at least a weapon," Drake thought to himself. However, he quickly ruled out the option of leaving as he heard Henderson roll to her side, moan, and unintelligibly whine. Leaving his concealed position along the wooded bank, he grabbed a large rock about the size of his own head and stalked up to the side of the canoe.

Peeking over the side wall of the boat with the rock extended in his arms, ready to slam it down on the deputy's head, Drake looked into her glossed over and distant eyes. She was already on her way out of this world. Drake decided smashing her skull was not needed and doing so in the boat could damage the bottom beyond repair. With his arms trembling from the pain of his bruise, Drake dropped the rock with a swift sigh of relief.

Thumping the side of the boat with his foot shook her motionless body just a bit and caused her to moan again. Reaching down into the boat, Drake removed the pistol from her holster and pointed it at her. Just as the rock would damage the boat, he knew a bullet would do the same. Having just killed Magee the night before with a firearm, Drake felt Henderson was deserving of a more honorable death. Tossing the gun out into the middle of the river, Drake decided he was done with shooting people.

Drake then placed his foot on the top edge of the boat and applied his body weight against it, causing the canoe to flip to its side and the deputy to roll out. Hitting the rocks and lying face down in four inches of river water caused Henderson to roll again to her back, this time with her eyes open, looking around in a panicked state.

Drake quickly grabbed her by the throat with his uninjured left hand, pulling her out into knee-deep water. Looking into her eyes as he held her head above the water, her limp body sank and the back of her ankles drug across the rocky river bed floor. The deputy's eyes remained open, but she was in a distant state. Unresponsive and seemingly unaware of her surroundings, she provided no resistance as Drake continued to drag her out into the river until icy flowing water was just under his waistline.

Looking at her, he could not help but think how killing a girl might feel different than doing the same to a man. Was it the right thing to do? Should he show her some form of mercy? Standing in the cold river, his mind was quickly made up as he thought back to all the whitetail does and black bear sows they harvested over the years. Their insides were no different than a buck or bruins. They fed, ran, lived, and tasted the same. Killing Henderson was no different than killing Magee, Ravizza or a trespassing hunter. Ending lives was part of their life now, and she was no different.

With his decision made, Drake grabbed her uniform lapels and pushed the deputy's head under the water. She briefly struggled, lightly shaking back and forth, but never with enough force to even come close to breaking the grip of Drake, who then pinned her down deeper beneath the oxygen-robbed surface. With the final exhaling bubbles leaving her drowning mouth and nose, Drake loosened his grip, letting the limp and lifeless body float up to the surface. Looking across the river, he was unsure of what to do with her. Letting her go to float down to Pine Run would alert the town, but it may also send a message. Dragging her back up river to burn her body would be too difficult of a task. His only choice was to leave her lie there on the bank and return with his brother later.

Drake spun the body around letting the current push her legs downstream. Grabbing the shirt and vest behind her neck, he dragged the waterlogged deputy against the flow to the shore. Once reaching land, he brought Henderson a few more feet out of the water to make certain her body would not float away.

Out of breath and suffering from the pain inside his lungs, Drake dropped to his hands and knees in an attempt to breathe, but a constant string of coughs would not let him do so. Each deep, gasping breath was answered by a raging, body-shaking cough that all but forced him to stay in a prone position for fear of passing out and falling face-first into the shallow bank side water. Each cough rocked his chest cavity to the point that the boy began to feel lightheaded.

Losing all sense of balance and sight from the combination of not being able to breathe and his level of pain, Drake rested on his side. With his shoulder resting in the water, Drake propped his head up on his forearm and continued coughing. He removed the hand covering his mouth to find it covered in a thick, frothy blood.

As he laid there struggling to breathe, coughing up blood into the river water, the irony of the situation was not missed. He thought about the fact that he had just drowned Henderson in the same river that was causing him to struggle to breathe. This may have been the same feeling she had as she looked up at him through the water.

It was also not lost on him that this time he was alone. Tomek was not there to save him as he had been many times before. In fact, he had not even told his twin about the canoe upon dashing out the door in a hurry. Uncle had died in the shallows of the river, and Drake knew it was a fitting place for him as well. His thoughts on the situation were much less clear with each failed attempt at catching any air that entered his now-burning lungs. The dizziness of the situation took its toll and upon losing consciousness, Drake's head, now unsupported by his arm, slumped down into the river.

Lying there face-down, drowning in four inches of water, his two remaining coughs did nothing but blow more blood from his lungs into the water. The current took the red stream downriver, away from what was to be his final resting place.

Coughing again while regaining brief consciousness, his face was now out of the water, but he felt and knew it was not him holding his head up. Slipping back in and out of the darkness that was his state of mind, he again woke up, this time lying on his back, having no idea how he had flipped over. Drake laid there, only knowing now that he was staring up at the blue sky. Taking in a deep breath for the first time in minutes without a cough, his eyes opened further to realize he was not, in fact, dead.

Sitting up, unaware and still dizzy, he looked around him, having no clue how much time had passed. While it had only been minutes, Drake felt as if he had been dead for hours. Shaking the water and blood from his hair, he placed his good left arm on the ground as a base in an attempt to rock sideways to his knee and stand up.

As quick as he had shifted his weight onto the arm, from the corner of his eye, we saw a sweeping leg fly in and kick his elbow, taking out his brace and causing his chest to slam back down, splashing into the river.

Unable to move before his assailant made its next attack, Drake laid there with an enemy on his back. Their knee was placed directly into the back of his shoulder, pushing his broken ribs into the rocky river bottom below where they grinded back and forth and all but immobilized him.

Feeling his head lift again, this time by his hair being pulled from behind, a tactical knife was placed at his throat. With the water line above his mouth, he continued to struggle breathing with his nostrils hovering in and out of the river. Looking down, he could see the sliver metal shine of the knife blade through the refracted water. If seeing the blade was not enough for him to realize he was about to be done in, feeling the cold metal pressed against his voice box was enough insurance for him to take his last breath in this world.

"I am alive, but I am ready to die. Do it!"

Drake urged the attacker to take his life and tried to assist by pushing his head downward onto the knife with all the force he could muster. Feeling the blade cutting into his skin, he closed his eyes and thought of Uncle.

Drake had always thought of Uncle's suicide as a cowardly act. Until this very moment when Drake knew his death was upon him, he realized that it is a not a coward who takes control of his own destiny. Rather it took bravery to face death, look him eye-to-eye, and then accept it as if greeting an old friend. Drake was not sure if he truly believed in this, or if it was his way of trying to convince himself that he was about to experience an honorable death.

"Kill me, kill me, kill me, kill me," he repeated over and over, willing the capturer to slice his throat.

Upon receiving an answer, if hearing the voice above him was not surprise enough, the words they spoke certainly were.

"I am not going to kill you...little brother," Deputy Henderson said. Henderson removed the blade, dropping him back into the river where he rolled over, sat up, and stared at her in silence.

19 One Left

As the tree-covered door to the underground cabin opened again, Tomek paid no attention, rolling over in his cot and pulling the covers up over his head. He was still somewhat talking in his sleep about finding the woman he had no idea was his own sister. The door left open on purpose was letting in both the cold air and light, both of which thoroughly annoyed Tomek enough for him to sit up in his cot, rub his eyes, and yell at his brother sitting at the table in the kitchen area.

"Close the freaking door, you ass!" Tomek said, lying back down and rolling over. No answer came from the kitchen area, and the door remained open.

Sitting back up, Tomek turned to again yell at his brother. Only it was not his brother at the table. The sheriff had invaded the cabin and stood there, gun drawn and looking at Tomek with a shit-eating grin. The next seconds went by in Tomek's mind as if they were days as he thought to himself, "*Is this the end? How did he find us? Where is Drake?*" all of which joined with many other racing thoughts into one large pile of confusion.

"Good morning, sunshine," the sheriff said.

Tomek did not answer, only looking at his captor with a burning fury in his eyes. How could he, how could *they,* have gotten trapped not only by Magee but now by the sheriff? Uncle had taught them better than this, and now the only place they knew to be safe was compromised. Tomek sat in his cot inside the very cabin that for all these years had protected him. The cabin had been safe from bears, wolves, storms, and even humans until this point. Now his safe zone had become his prison.

"I know you can talk, son," the sheriff said. "Better say something, or I am going to have to make ya talk the hard way."

"I am not your fucking son."

"That's more like it. Now where is that little look-alike spook brother of yours? You know, the one who likes to sneak around fires and kill dogs."

Again, Tomek did not answer the sheriff but the question did bring some ease to heart. He now knew that unless the invader was trying to trick him, Drake had not been taken or killed.

"He's dead," Tomek said with pain in his voice, trying to cover the lie. "One of your piece of shit buddies gunned him down from far off like he was nothing but an animal."

Tomek had decided if he was about to die at the hands of the sheriff, it was better for the sheriff to think that Drake was dead as well.

"An animal, huh? Look at you boys, running in the woods, living in a hole under the ground. That is exactly what you maggots are: stinky, dirty, dark-skinned ... animals."

Tomek, not realizing the full extent to which he was being insulted, looked into the eyes of his enemy and said, "Go ahead and kill me like an animal, then. Sneak up on me in my sleep and take me out. It is better than dying like my brother did from a far-off cowardly shot."

"Ahh, good ol' boy Magee got 'em with the trusty rifle, eh?" the sheriff said. "Well, as much as I do like your version of the story there, junior, it's just not true. See, I done watched you two cross the river together last night after tracking down the sound of that rifle letting one loose."

The sheriff calling Tomek's bluff was not at all what he wanted to hear. The sheriff knowing Drake was alive took away the only strategy Tomek had at protecting his brother from the grave.

The sheriff strolled casually around the small cabin, keeping Tomek at gunpoint while he continued his diatribe regaling the events of last night from his point of view.

"That river is mighty cold this time of the year, and I'll admit it was funny as hell seeing you both in it. Now because you two little freaks look damn near the same, I don't know who knocked who in, but either way, yeah, it was funny."

"Whatever ..." Tomek answered.

"I see how it is. You're just like any other little punk kid we deal with. You can take the punk out of Pine Run, but you can't take the Pine Run out of the punk," the sheriff said.

"I have never even been to Pine Run, so there goes that theory," Tomek boasted, as he clearly did not get the sentiment of the lawman's point.

"I'll have to call your bluff once more there, son," the sheriff said, reaching down the front of his shirt and pulling out the arrowhead that was found buried in the shoulder of the elk that caused his accident all those years ago. The sheriff had wrapped the head in a leather strand and wore it is a necklace for years as a reminder of that fateful day.

"I am not your damn son," Tomek scolded again.

Upon seeing the hand-chipped flint stone arrowhead necklace that the sheriff was now dangling in front of him, Tomek immediately knew it was made by Uncle.

"Did the man holding him at gunpoint know Uncle?" Tomek wondered.

Silently, the minutes continued to pass as Tomek just sat in the cot listening to the gentle flow of the river splashing against the rock-sided bank. The sheriff quietly wandered about the small room, tearing apart the cabin's nooks and crannies as if he was looking for something.

"What y'all got to eat around this place?" the sheriff asked as he walked toward the kitchen cupboards. Looking back at Tomek, he shrugged his shoulders and opened his palms in a gesture that demanded an answer.

"Well, boy, I ain't talking to myself," he said.

Tomek again did not answer verbally; he just nodded in an upward fashion toward the cupboards where the supplies and rations were kept. Most of what remained were the canned vegetables from last year's crops. Grabbing a sealed glass jar from the front of the shelf, the sheriff held it up to the light now coming in through the sky vent.

"Pickles, huh?"

"Yup," Tomek answered.

"Dill or sweet?"

"Dill, picked right from our own garden," Tomek said in an attempt to make the snack sound more enticing, knowing full well the particular jar that was now open on the table contained the deadly poison of Death Angel mushrooms and Nightshade berries. The rule of *After 5, Stay Alive* might just save him by taking out the sheriff without even a hint of a struggle.

Picking the jar back up and holding it his nose, the sheriff smelled the contents with a long drawn in breath through his nostrils. Smiling, he dipped his fingers down in to the jar, grabbed a pickle, and removed it almost all the way from the jar where he bumped it on the side of the glass to knock off the excess drips of juice.

"Sure hope they are still crunchy," the sheriff said as he held it up to his lips. Opening his mouth, Tomek watched with anticipation of what would happen next. The sheriff placed the pickle between his teeth and began to bite down. While looking at Tomek, however, he sensed something was strange in the boy's behavior. Removing the still-intact pickle from his mouth, he flipped it over to Tomek, where it landed in his lap.

"How rude of me. I should have offered you a last meal," the sheriff said.

"You're not going to kill me, just the way Ravizza couldn't kill me,"

Tomek answered.

Looking at Tomek, the sheriff plucked another pickle from the jar and placed it in his mouth, holding it in his teeth as if it was a cigar. Little did he know how deadly of a cigar it would be if just one bite was taken.

"So you met Ravizza, huh? As good with the stars as he is, I'm sure he's back in Pine Run by now. Warm and waiting for us to all return laughing about that damn cougar."

"Nope," Tomek said with a sinister smile. "He is over in the pines, just west of the orchard near the river's edge."

"He set up some sort of a camp, huh? Well, he is an adventuresome guy," the sheriff said.

"Nope," again Tomek said, smiling. "Well, maybe he is camping. If lying on a bed of pine needles naked with a hatchet buried in your skull being fed upon by the buzzards and coyotes is considered camping, then yeah, he is camping."

The sheriff knew by Tomek's confident tone that this time there was no bluff. The pickle dropped from his clenched teeth as he raised his gun up at Tomek. "You black devil son of a bitch. You can't just kill people and expect to go on about your ways. These people have lives."

"Had lives," Tomek interrupted.

"These people have families," the sheriff continued.

"Had families," Tomek again corrected, this time standing up and inching toward the sheriff slowly. "Ravizza is dead just like the wolf he brought with him and that big troll-like fool is dead as well. My brother had no problem killing your good ol' boy Magee, and your little black bitch is dead, too. In fact, you, sheriff, you are the only one left, so kill me now, but know he will find you."

Tomek continued, still inching closer and closer as he continued to bravely berate the person holding him captive at gunpoint.

"My brother will avenge me, my brother will hunt you, my brother will hurt you, my brother will kill everything precious to you. First, your wife, your life, your blood and then, and only then, once your life has been ruined, it will be taken."

Now standing just on the other side of the table, Tomek picked up the pickle jar, shaking it at the sheriff with each point he made, spilling its contents about the table and room.

"Uncle taught us in order to win a war, you must make the citizen feel as if his government cannot protect him anymore. You, sheriff, may kill me, but you have lost this war as you can no longer protect the few who look to you for help. Your men are dead, your woman is dead, and your wolf is dead. Soon you will join them."

"Ya done yet?" the sheriff asked, shrugging off Tomek's threats of retribution.

The fact that he was seemingly unaffected by Tomek's words enraged Tomek. How could a man who has or soon will have lost it all not care? It was at this point that Tomek decided to go on the offensive. His original plan of dying easily at the hands of the sheriff to go on as a martyr for Drake was no longer an option for two reasons. First, if the sheriff wanted to kill him, he would have done so already. The sheriff must have wanted to take him back to Pine Run in custody as some kind of a human trophy. The second reason, simply put, is that it was not within his personality or training to lie down and die.

With the decision made to fight, Tomek threw the glass jar forward, launching the remaining pickle juice into the face of the sheriff and kicked the edge of the table top pushing it forcefully back into the thighs of his enemy. The juice to the face was enough to distract the sheriff, allowing the impact of the table to slam into him before he was able to brace for it. Falling face-first and hunched over the table, which now had him pinned against the back wall of the sink area, the sheriff lifted his head as he raised his gun, aiming for Tomek. The shot rattled both Tomek and the sheriff's eardrums as the sound of the blast echoed harshly inside the small cabin walls.

Missing his intended target from mere yards away, the round had sailed over Tomek's head as he slid on his side, much in the manner he would have if he ever needed to enter the pine slider. The sheriff fired again into the table trying to hit Tomek as he was underneath it, but to no avail. Sliding from the front of the table underneath to the back, Tomek popped up with a razor-sharp, stone-tipped knife only he knew was stored beneath the edge of the table.

Now with Tomek standing behind the sheriff's right hip, the sheriff turned his head in time to dodge the knife strike that was intended for the throat. Tomek's attack was not a total failure as the knife's jagged blade sliced its way right through both cheeks and opened the sheriff's face as if it was the belly of a deer. With his movement still restricted by the heavy table, he turned to face Tomek. The skin-deep facial wound allowed the sheriff to briefly ignore the gushing blood that was rushing down his throat from what were the corners of his mouth and cheeks. They now flapped loose and hung down his jawline exposing his bottom teeth.

Coughing up blood, the sheriff attempted to raise his gun but stumbled forward, dizzily bracing himself with his hand against the table. The knife's impact was so smooth, it was not even felt. Tomek had buried the blade deep into the top of the table, going straight through the sheriff's hand, causing the gun to be released. This final blow was enough to send the heavily bleeding man into shock, and he again slumped forward atop the table, unconscious.

Tomek admired the man as he laid there, proud of the handiwork he had just completed. Proud of the fact that only ten minutes prior, he had decided to die, looked death in the face, and defeated him on his own accord. Walking over to the table, he saw the gun sitting there. Picking it up, he placed the barrel to the back of the sheriff's head and pulled the trigger.

"Click."

As the hammers firing pin clashed against the empty chamber, Tomek realized that not a single round remained in the weapon. Knowing he had plenty of rounds remaining from the other weapons they had scavenged, he turned to retrieve one. It would only take one.

Turning around meant he never saw the glass pickle jar hit him in the back of the head. The impact shattered the jar into pieces, causing multiple cuts to both Tomek's neck and the sheriff's hand. Tomek lunged forward, crashing into his bed where his head impacted the corner, and he was out. No bright lights, no dizziness, no flashes, just out. Unconscious and lying on the ground vulnerable, this was the sheriff's only chance and he knew it.

Grasping onto the handle of the handmade knife that connected his body to the tabletop, the sheriff attempted to pull it up and out of the table. Unsuccessful due to his hand slipping from the blood on the weapon and the depth that the blade had driven down into the top, the sheriff knew he had only one option left.

Bleeding hard with continuous blood pouring from both the wounds on his face and right hand, he removed the belt from his pants and wrapped it around his right wrist. Once tight enough to restrict the blood flow, and after a series of deep, clear inhaled breaths, the sheriff grabbed onto his right wrist. He then pulled his hand back with all the weight his body could muster for leverage and watched as the leading edge of the blade left above the table sliced its way through the rest of his hand, exiting between his middle and ring finger. The belt had done its job, and this new gash, that had left his blue hand looking much like the claw of a crawfish, hardly bled. What he had saved in blood he made up for in pain as his body flickered in and out of shock.

Holding the severed hand up into his chest, he wiggled free of the table top and stood over Tomek's body. Looking around the room for some sort of a weapon, the sheriff's eyes glanced to the cubby where Tomek had placed the pistol that belonged to Magee. Working toward the other side of the room, dragging his feet along the blood-soaked dirt floor, the sheriff kept his eyes focused on the gun in an attempt to not pass out.

Losing his sense of balance once reaching the wall, he fell to his knees. Unable to breathe through his mouth due to the stone knife's damage, the sheriff forced himself to inhale deeply through his nostrils. Looking down, he was able to gain his composure. Unable to stand yet, at the base of the wall and still down on one knee, he reached up over his head, feeling around inside the cubby for the pistol he hoped was loaded.

As his outstretched fingers crawled up and over the bottom edge of the cubby, the cold feeling of the black polymer grip belonging to the gun was a sigh of relief. Knowing that if the gun was loaded, he would be able to take out Tomek and at least he would be alive for now. The thought of Drake's location, as well as how the sheriff planned to escape back to Pine Run with his injuries, were bridges he planned to cross once he got there. Now, in this moment, all that mattered to him was killing his way back out of the underground cabin.

Reaching in and lifting the gun up was enough movement to trigger the covered bear leg hold trap under the weapon. The very reason Drake had originally told Tomek to be careful placing the pistol in the cubby to begin with was that they both new what was beneath the false dirt floor of the small . Using the gun as bait had worked perfectly, as the spring-loaded rusty iron tension-loaded claws slammed forcefully shut on the lawman's arm.

The trap's teeth buried themselves into his flesh, only stopping once they reached bone. With his entire arm, from elbow to wrist, caught in a trap that was meant to hold a bear in place, the sheriff was going nowhere. Still, the force of the deathly jaws slamming onto his arm shocked his system to the point where he sprung up to his feet. With the pain releasing every last bit of endorphins left in his body, the sheriff sprinted toward Tomek's lifeless form.

Connected to the base of every bear trap the boys had ever set was a holding chain that is staked into the ground, and this trap was no different. If the power of a 400-pound black bear was not enough to pull the trap stake loose, the sheriff certainly did not stand a chance at reaching Tomek. Lunging away from the wall cubby, the sheriff began to move across the room. Three steps later, the chain pulled taut, digging the teeth deeper into his arm, separating the bones from their connective tendons.

The sheriff's forward momentum being suddenly jerked back forced his feet out from under him and up into the air, where gravity joined along with the effectiveness of the chain stake in slamming the man back onto the hard-packed dirt floor. Lying on the ground, with his outstretched trapped arm above his head, the sheriff looked up one last time.

Pushing his heels against the ground and trying to move backward toward the wall to regain his balance, much like Ravizza did on the pine needle-covered floor, the sheriff reached the cubby wall again where he sat up leaning his back against it. Looking across the room, with the only light coming in from the oak tree door cracked open a few inches and a single flickering candle on the counter top, the sheriff nodded up and down as his level of consciousness drifted in and out.

Staring at a still-motionless Tomek, the sheriff began laughing. Not a silent chuckle to himself about the improbability of the situation he was in, but a full roaring maniac's laugh. The full-breathed guttural cackles were met with blood spouting out of his torn-apart mouth with each burst. His cheeks now resembled loose flaps of skin now covered in a bloody mud made from the dirt picked up during his impact with the floor.

The combination of his wounds eventually overcame him and on his biggest laugh, the sheriff gathered all the air in his lungs to yell at Tomek, "You can't kill me!"

Upon finishing the words, he slumped back into the wall, his head dropping to the floor as his body fell away from the cubby. Lying there with his face on the ground between his legs, ear to the dirt, with his right arm held up in the air by the tension of the chain, the sheriff's gruesome battle with Tomek was over.

20 Family

"My sister?"

"Yes, I am your sister, only you don't remember me," she said. "It was so long ago, and you were so young. My ... *our* father had moved me away and was soon coming to get you when she, our mother, that is, vanished," Henderson said, while stepping toward Drake.

Drake was unsure what bothered him the most. Was it the fact that what she said might be true, or was it that for some reason he believed her?

"You have to be lying. Uncle told us ... me about our ... *my* mother," Drake said, poorly attempting to hide Tomek's existence.

Looking at her long-lost younger brother, the deputy extended her hand. "I don't know who this Uncle is, but if he saved you two, then I want to thank him. For all these years we thought you were gone or, even worse, dead," Henderson said.

"*Us two*?" Drake replied, trying to keep up the charade that he was alone in the woods.

"Yes, your brother. Please, God, tell me you know you had, *have* a twin. He was different. You could see it in his left eye," Henderson said, referring to Tomek's left blue eye while his right one was green, like Drake's.

Stepping closer again to Drake, Henderson looked into his green eyes. "My name is Annette. Do you remember me at all?"

"No," said Drake.

"What about your brother or our parents?" asked Henderson.

"No," said Drake. "Uncle never would have lied."

"Your brother's name was–"

"His name is Tomek," Drake said, cutting her off. He knew that hearing his brother's birth name would be too much to handle in his state.

"Is he alive?" his sister asked.

Unable to speak, Drake only nodded. The rush of new information about his life was more than he could take. Had he just slammed the rock down on her head, he would be on his way back to the warm cabin. Yet, no. Now he rested on the rocks of the river bank, wet, cold, and sore, pondering his existence in these woods. He spent the next few minutes thinking silently, as Henderson continued to provide him with info about their life before Uncle. Every bit of it was about things she would have had no other way of knowing. It was clear to him they had not swayed far from the personalities they had as toddlers.

"Was everything Uncle had told them untrue?"

"How could she have known so much about them and not be telling the truth?"

"What will Tomek say?"

It did start to make some form of sense. From the moment the twins set eyes on the deputies days before, Henderson was a constant topic of discussion. Drake and Tomek had both talked about how there was something about her. While Tomek's motive was most likely more violent, Drake thought that the female deputy's presence was more important than the others. However, until now, he had no idea why. Drake had figured it was most likely the fact that she was a female. He also knew her skin color was the same as his, which was a new experience for both of the twins.

Uncle had taught them that nature adapts and prevails in hopeless situations. Much like the flow of a river will round the edges of stone, nature will take you and change you as well.

"Is she the new stone in our river?"

"Could she be shaped to fight, survive, and live their lifestyle?"

Breaking his train of thought was her hand on his shoulder shaking him back to reality.

"Can you take me to our brother?"

Drake was startled by her touch. In his state of lifeless daydreaming, he never observed her getting close to him. He knew that if she wanted him dead at this point, he would have been. Reaching under his arms and lifting him up to his feet, she pulled him close to her body in an embrace.

The simple hug, with her hand on the back of his neck holding his head on her shoulder, instantly dumped a rush of emotions that, for some reason, calmed him. The strange presence of these feelings made him almost subconsciously hold her tighter. In his sister's arms, Drake felt safe for the first time since Uncle's December death. Holding Henderson as if he was never going to let go, Drake realized that since learning he had a sister, whether it was true or not, he wanted it to be real.

Leaning back from the boy and running her hand across his head, she continued to ask him questions.

"How did you survive?"

"What do you remember?"

"Who is Uncle?"

Rubbing his hand across his swollen ribcage, in between coughs, he struggled to talk in full sentences. "Let's head back to Tomek. I have a lot to tell you," Drake said as he reached out for the short rope tied to the front of the canoe, pulling it up onto the rock bed in order to secure it for a later time when they could come and retrieve it.

As the bottom of the handmade boat grinded across the rock ledge shore, Drake looked at this woman, this person who was now, apparently, also his sister. He did not see her as a threat, as an enemy, or as one of Uncle's dreaded government officials. Henderson was just a girl, a survivor, one of them. Drake knew he had come to this conclusion much too quickly, and his brother would never be so easily swayed. For that reason, he decided it was best for her to know as much about their way of life, before and after Uncle's death, as possible.

"Yes, please take me to him. I want to meet him and learn more about you both. All these years our father has said you were both dead, but somehow I knew different. All these years later I moved back to Pine Run, and here you are. The guys are not going to believe this."

"Guys?" Drake asked.

Henderson continued, "Yeah, the guys I work with. We got separated when a cougar attacked us two days ago. I've heard a few gun shots, and I've been trying to work my way back toward them. When I found the boat, I figured I would float to town and meet back up with them. Only I found you instead. This is amazing! This is a miracle."

Weak and cold, Drake was not sure that informing his new found sibling of how her little brothers had systematically taken the lives of each of her fellow officers was a good idea. However, he knew that she would eventually find out, and it may be better for him to tell her than Tomek. He half expected Tomek to boast about each one's death, and only having known his sister for twenty-five minutes, he was unsure about the reaction that may bring. As they walked back, Drake began the short version of a long story. He explained to the deputy how they were raised, how they hunt, trap, grow, and survive.

Reaching the whale rock, which was now fully exposed thanks to the river's waterlevel dropping, Drake sat down to rest. With the sun raised fully into the early morning sky, the warmth of the rock's surface was a welcome change from his wet shirt. Lying down on his back, the pressure seemed to lift off of his rib cage, which provided temporary relief. As his constant coughing subsided, lying next to him, with her head propped up on her hand, he did not see Henderson as a cop and actually cracked a smile. The thought still flabbergasted him, yet for some reason he was at peace with Henderson. Drake knew he was trained to hate her, but he did not.

"What happened to your chest?" Henderson asked him.

"I was shot, with a rifle, in the dark and from a distance," he said.

"What? Who in the hell shot you, and how are you alive?" Henderson said, sitting up with concern on her face.

"Well, his name tag, like yours, said Magee."

"Magee does not miss. You obviously were hit with something," she continued to prod, asking only open-ended questions the way she would with any normal investigation she would handle as a detective.

"He did not miss at all; he hit me clear as can be right here over my heart."

"How are you alive?" she asked.

"You cannot kill what is not alive," Drake said trying to steal his brother's line. Henderson did not flinch. The line had a much better effect on Magee in the last moments of his life, but Henderson was not buying it. She only looked at him and continued on with her questioning.

"Horse shit. You're not going to get all mystical on me," Henderson said. "How ... are you ... alive?" his sister asked with a serious tone, this time demanding a proper answer.

"The tan skin one who had the dog is dead. I used his heavy coat and vest to shield my chest. Magee shot me and knocked me down, Tomek surprised him, and while they were fighting, I got back up and killed him."

154

Drake retold the story with no emotion and no regret while looking her straight in the eyes. With all her training and experience over the years, she knew he was telling the truth. She also knew that only true sociopaths could recall their violent acts in such a manner.

Although society would clearly label anyone who killed without any regard to right and wrong like him a sociopath, she was not so sure. Was it that her brothers were truly evil, or was it the fact that they were raised in the wild? Was it nature or nurture? After all, the snake does not feel sorrow for the mouse.

Henderson stood silent and stunned. Truthfully, though, she felt almost glad Magee was dead in place of either of her brothers. If she found them after all these years only to learn that one or both of them had been killed by a fellow officer, it would be torture. Henderson knew she was looking at a killer. Henderson knew Drake was a person who society, the law, and all her clinical training would deem a sociopath. Yet for some reason, all she saw was her little brother, who did not know any better and was trained to commit these horrible acts. Looking at him, unafraid, she asked about Ravizza.

"The tan one is Ravizza. How did you get his coat?" she asked.

Sitting up to look at her, he casually remarked, "Ravizza, as you call him, had Tomek in handcuffs at gun point."

"And?" she asked again, leaving the conversation open in an attempt to extract more from the boy.

"Ravizza is dead, just like his dog, just like the big blond ignorant giant and just like ..."

"I am going to be?" she interrupted to ask.

"No," Drake said. "I will protect you."

Rolling her eyes at the thought of her little sixteen-year-old brother operating as her protection was somewhat comical to hear. Although the more they sat there and he explained Tomek to her, the more she understood. Henderson was clearly beginning to see the dynamic between her twin brothers and was grateful that it was Drake who found her in the boat and not Tomek.

As time passed by, the pair continued back toward the cabin. Drake figured she had no idea of its location, so he meandered through the wood line and the orchard in order to spend just a few more minutes alone with Henderson. Although his body was hurting with each step and breath, he figured as soon as they met up with Tomek, circumstances would change so drastically that he wanted to enjoy the time he still had alone with her.

Making their way down through the hillside garden area he explained how they picked their fruit and stored it in the dry cellar. Henderson was impressed with both the orchard and their sophisticated pit-protected garden plot. She was less impressed with the beehive colony the twins and uncle had cultivated over time.

"Keep those things away from me. One sting and I'm dead," she said.

"Tomek shares your reaction to the sting, but over the years Uncle used many plants and oils to build up Tomek's resistance to the venom. Now if he gets stung, only the wound gets infected. However, if we make a plant remedy from the common plantain weed and place it on the sting spot, it will cure it in a few hours," Drake explained, trying to impress his sister with his woodland medical knowledge—a feat at which he was successful, based on that fact that Henderson felt safer in the presence of the bees with Drake by her side.

"They are good for honey, obviously, and they keep the gardens and orchards pollinated. We live as one with them. The only difference being that the hive has a queen, and we never have. Until now," Drake said.

Henderson again was taken aback by how clear and on point Drake's speech was. It wasn't that he was a well-taught classical English speaker. Even more so, it was not what he said. It was the way he said it. Straight to the point and without emotion was what she had come to expect from him. This made her wonder if Tomek would be the same way.

"Wow, you don't sugarcoat anything do you?" Henderson asked.

"Sugarcoat?" Drake did not understand the phrase.

"Never mind. It's just a saying," Henderson replied.

It was in this moment that Henderson began to really question herself on what their future together would entail. For all intents and purposes, it was clear Drake wanted her to stay with them and assimilate into their way of life. Honestly, she knew that would be difficult but was open-minded enough to see that it was possible from a pure survival standpoint. They had the skills to live on their own. Food, water, and weapons were not a problem. She had not seen their shelter, yet even though at this point they had walked directly past it four times. Each time, Drake smiling as they strolled on by the oak tree door.

"Could she live with them?"

"Who would come looking for us?"

"They are cop killers. They will have to answer for their crimes, won't they?"

All of the above raced through her mind. Would Pine Run ever know the truth? There was certainly no way everyone would just accept that the entire Sheriff's Department mysteriously went missing in the woods. She was sure search parties would come and then it dawned on her: She was, in fact, herself part of a search party. She was the last remaining part of one, for that matter. If Henderson stayed with her brothers and became one of them, would she have to hide? Or would more drastic options be the only way to prolong their way of life?

Walking in circles for the last two hours, she realized Drake was attempting to stall the reunion with Tomek. Just as she began to speak up about it, Drake stopped walking along the river bank and turned toward what looked to her to be a blown-down tree lofted along the hillside. Following the boy's lead, she stretched her legs and hopped from rock to rock just as Drake did.

"Is this some kind of test?" she asked him.

"Nope," he said.

"Why are we jumping from rock to rock then?"

"Do you see the taller switch grass from the river up to that tree?"

he asked.

"Of course," she said, still a little annoyed.

"Well, if there was a path trampled through it, then someone might follow that path, wouldn't you think?" Drake asked fatuously.

"I suppose," his sister said.

"I am taking you to our home, your home, and this is how we approach it. This keeps us hidden from random people floating down our river. This is how we live. This was all Uncle's idea," Drake said while leaping to the last rock.

Standing at the tree trunk, it was still not obvious to her that it was a door. Although, as Drake rotated a false piece of the bark aside, she was quickly amazed at the intricate handle that had been carved into the body of the tree.

Opening the door exposed to her a sight she could never have imagined. There on the floor lay the second of her twin brothers. She rushed into the dimly lit room and dropped to her knees and picked up Tomek. Pulling his limp body into her lap and arms she was astounded at the true likeness both boys shared. Further relived to see he was still breathing, Henderson was taken aback as she looked over his shoulder.

She knew her fellow deputies had been killed but was unprepared to see any one of their particular bodies. Seeing the sheriff's body was also something she had not expected, yet there he was, standing over her, alive and chained to the wall via the bear trap looking at her for mercy.

21 Decisions

"Annette, look what they have done to me," the sheriff said, referencing his current bloodied disposition.

"We've done nothing to you yet!" yelled Drake. This was the first time he himself had been face-to-face with the leader of the trespassers.

"The events of the last two days have been because of your actions. You came here, you attacked, you trespassed, all the while never telling our sister what you truly were coming for. Every man you dragged out here is dead because of you."

"Your sister?" the sheriff asked, looking down to the ground in disbelief. "Do you honestly think this bitch is your sister? Your mother was a drugged-out whore, and you both should have died beside her in that truck."

Henderson laid Tomek down softly on the ground and stood to look her boss directly in the face. "You know how they vanished? You know about her truck? You knew she was dead? That was my mother, *our* mother."

"Oh, are we playing a little charade that you're the long-lost sister these two somehow never knew about?" he sarcastically asked. "Hell yes, I knew she was dead. I'm the one who found the damn truck. Full of cargo fresh out of the Canadian pharmacy headed into town," the sheriff said. "That bitch was working for the wrong guy. I needed the meds, not the truck, or those damn twins. I figured someone would find it and oh, the fucking tragedy it would be. But nope, years later, and not a single hiker tripped upon it. Somehow it remained my little secret. I went back to check it out one time, but it was gone—poof!—fucking vanished."

"She was alive?" Drake asked from the corner of the room, stepping into the light coming through the open door.

The sheriff looked up upon hearing Drake's voice. "Damn, I had hoped they would have killed at least one of you demons."

"She was alive?" Henderson asked with the same intensity in her voice.

"Like I said, I needed the meds, not the whore!" the sheriff said.

Standing side by side, Drake and Henderson both reached for one of the flint-napped blades sitting on the shelf beside them. The stone blades were nowhere as strong as one of Drake's preferred throwing knives, but the hollowed-out slice in the sheriff's hand could attest that they were just as sharp.

Bumping into one another, Henderson gave way to her little brother as he picked up the blade and took a step toward the sheriff, who was now dropped down on one knee.

Looking up at what seemed like just a boy above him ready to end his life, he said, "You know, she's not your sister. Uncle could never have hidden a sister from you."

Hearing the name Uncle escape from the tattered remnants of the sheriff's cheek flaps caused Drake to step back.

"I found you in that truck, the both of you. I gave you to your precious Uncle and in return, he presented me with this necklace. As long as I stayed away from him and let him go, that was the deal. And this bitch ... is not your sister. Her momma was the only black bitch in town. A nurse, if I remember correctly. Not a whore like your mother," the sheriff said, gasping between each word.

The sheriff was dying on the spot from the overwhelming blood loss from the injuries he sustained fighting Tomek, but he was still able to spin a lie. The major issue being that each statement held a shred of possible truth.

"He knows about Uncle and is wearing a head Uncle made on his neck. How could he know about the truck and how Uncle had found them? There was a black nurse when I was in the hospital. Is Annette my sister?" Drake thought to himself.

"He's lying, Drake. I loved you boys more than anything, and I have been searching for you all my life," Henderson said.

The sheriff chuckled.

Amidst all the confusion and discussion between the three of them, Tomek remained lying on the floor. Stepping over his body to get closer to Drake, Henderson reached out her hand.

"We don't have to kill him," Drake said. This comment made both the sheriff and Henderson alike raise their heads in confusion. Neither of them had expected any type of mercy to be shown.

"Drake is right. We don't have to kill him," Tomek said, looking at Henderson. Drake stepped back toward his brother, who was now standing in an attempt to get between Tomek and Henderson.

"I have a lot to tell you. I know it may sound crazy, but this is—"

"Our sister," Tomek said, interrupting his brother.

"What, you knew?" Henderson asked.

"Yes," Tomek replied.

Drake was now in the state of confusion he had expected Tomek to be upon learning about Henderson.

"How?" Drake asked.

"Uncle," Tomek said. "I knew it was her from the minute we saw them at their first camp with the wolf."

"You've been trying to kill her from the get go," Drake said.

"No, save her," Tomek corrected his brother. "Uncle told me about her, told me there was another one of us and that one day she may come looking for us."

"When?" Drake asked.

"You were sick in the hospital at Pine Run. You were supposed to either die there or be taken from us. He did not expect you to ever return to our life, and he said I should never feel alone because if you died, there would still be one more of us. He told me there was a girl, Annette, and she would be older."

"Why didn't you tell me?" Drake asked.

"To see that look on your face. Ha, and now I am glad I waited."

Tomek's answer annoyed his brother, but Drake was not surprised by it.

"So no, we don't have to kill him," Tomek said, taking a breath. "We don't, but she does."

"Wait, what?" Henderson asked.

Tomek remained silent and walked over to the sheriff, pushing him down to the floor. Tomek reached into the cubby and pulled out the pistol the sheriff had attempted to obtain when his hand wound up in the clutches of the bear trap.

Continuing his silent but deliberate movement across the room, he opened a pull-out drawer from the cabinetry near where their beds would have normally been before his scuffle with the sheriff. Removing a single round from the drawer, he walked over to Henderson and handed her both the gun and bullet. Tomek then looked at her intensely and said, "Kill him. Kill him and prove you are one of us."

Henderson looked at her younger brother, knowing this was the moment that Drake was trying to prepare her for during the conversation on the walk back to the cabin. It was at this point she knew it would be the sheriff's life or her own, and if she did not take his, the boys would take them both. Looking back at Drake for some semblance of understanding, she was surprised to see him with the same look as Tomek.

Both boys stood side by side, strong, united; identical in every way except for Tomek's blue eye and Drake's damaged ear lobe. There they stood, as if a line had been drawn in the blood-soaked dirt floor. Kill her boss or become like him. She had no other options, no way to talk herself out of the terror. This was either the end of her life or the start of a new one.

"It is the only way, sister," Drake said in a comforting manner.

"You are not a murderer, Annette. Do not become one of them. Shoot one of them and shoot them now!" the sheriff yelled.

Tomek raised his voice to overpower the sheriff. "There is no hunting like the hunting of man, and those who have hunted armed men long enough and like it never care for anything else thereafter."

"Stealing lines from Nietzsche only makes you a murderer and a thief," the sheriff said, laughing at what he thought was Tomek's attempt at sounding bright.

Unfazed by the sheriff's insult, Tomek put his finger inside of the gash of the sheriff's cheek, forcing his finger down into the man's throat. Grasping the side of the man's ripped-apart face, he pulled the struggling sheriff's ear up to his mouth, as if to tell him a secret.

"It's Hemingway, asshole," Tomek said.

Having made his point, Tomek dropped the man and walked over to his sister.

"It's time for us to be together again, to live as a family, the way Uncle always wanted. But first this retched puke must die. Are you ready?"

"I can't," she said. Tomek thought the pain in her voice was evidence that while she did want to be with them, bringing herself to murder her boss was not something she could accept.

"That is unfortunate," Drake said, as he reached down, pulling the stone-bladed knife from out of the tabletop where it had sliced through the sheriff's hand earlier.

"Then you understand, this is the end for you both. Do not fight, do not struggle, and you will die in peace," Tomek said.

"Would you like to say something to God?" Drake asked her.

"No, I never trusted religion because it teaches you to be okay without understanding the world in which you live," said Henderson.

"Good point," the sheriff said, now lying down on his side with the bear trap atop of his opposite arm.

"I think you're missing my point, little boys."

Not keen on being referred to as little boys, they allowed her to continue.

"I said I can't, not *I won't*." She held up both the gun and the single round of ammunition. "This is a forty-caliber round and a nine-millimeter pistol. You might not know much about these types of weapons, but just so we are clear, these two do not work together."

Her dramatic flair for informing them of Tomek's mistake had almost gotten her killed, but in all honesty, Drake loved it. For what had been the tensest moment in their past few days of surviving and taking lives, this moment was perfectly contrasted with the sense of relief in knowing now his sister was on their side. Tomek was less amused as he handed her the only round of forty-caliber ammunition they had in the entire cabin.

"Take this and end him, or end yourself," said Tomek.

"We will be at the river. Join us after you make your decision," Drake said, walking out of the cabin. Tomek was caught off guard by his brother leaving her alone with the sheriff, but knew his brother's plan without having to be told and followed him out of the cabin.

Once outside, with the door shut behind them, Drake looked at Tomek, and it was if they both could hear Uncle's voice.

"This hole is your home, your castle. Just as the mouse lives in a hole of his own, you must keep it a secret. If the snake finds the hole, the snake knows where to hunt. Only the mouse knows how to escape his own hole if stuck, and he is lucky that snakes do not hunt together for this gives him a chance. Use this hole as a weapon, as a trap if you must, but always hunt together. Be the snake, not the mouse."

And with that they both rolled the large boulder just uphill from the door off of its perch. It took both of them using their entire body weight to get it rolling. Landing on top of the oak tree door, it lodged into place, securing the door against the side of the hill. The cabin was now a prison with Henderson alone inside with the sheriff and only one round of ammunition.

"What now?" Tomek asked. Drake knew that at this point it was a waiting game.

"Let's go fishing," Drake said, jokingly.

"Ah, man, my fly rod is still inside," Tomek joked.

Jumping from rock to rock towards the river they both looked back at the door to their home.

"But really, what now?" Tomek again asked his brother and was not surprised with the shortness of the answer he was given.

"We wait."

22 Choices

"They left you here, trapped to rot and die in this underground prison. I cannot believe you didn't kill one of them while you had the fucking chance. Congratulations, Annette. You got outsmarted and left to die, slowly, by a couple of sixteen-year-olds."

"Says the grown-ass man chained to the wall with half a face," she replied.

Wanting to prove him wrong, Henderson walked over to the door, trying to open it in order to see just what exactly her brothers had done as they walked out. She had heard the thud the boulder made upon its impact, not to mention the dust that shook loose from the ceiling as it fell into place.

"I am dead. Look at me. I'll be done in a few hours. But you? Nope. You will be wasting away for days. Starving, dying slowly in this pit. This pit is where they left your ass. This is where you will suffer and die. Sure, you may have some food in here to live a while, but after that you will fade away into nothing."

"Can't eat the food. It's all been poisoned. Or at least some of it has," Henderson said.

"You sure about that? My pickle was delicious," the sheriff said, hiding the fact he hadn't actually eaten the boys' food.

"Yes, Drake told me. Well, no, I guess I'm not sure." The doubts about everything Drake had told her began to grow. Drake had said Tomek was the one she needed to worry about, but Tomek accepted her right away. Drake was the first to walk out of the cabin. Drake was the one who led her to the cabin in a roundabout way so she would not know the direct path. It began to become clearer to her with each passing realization. Drake was the reason she was trapped; Drake had fooled her and had done so easily.

Unable to prove her boss wrong, the overwhelming feeling of being trapped started to set in upon the female deputy. The room, still dark with only the still burning beeswax candles, began to feel smaller and smaller by the minute. Henderson franticly walked down the passageways dug into the hillside, avoiding the pitfall traps that Drake had told her about, all of which led to dead ends.

Returning to the living quarters, she kicked the sheriff's foot to see if he was still alive.

"What the hell? I'm not going anywhere, you dumb bitch," the sheriff said, very much still somehow alive. "You find any more rounds?"

"No," she said.

"So just the one, huh? Smart little shits they turned out to be," he said. "You know what you have to do, Annette. I am done. We are done, but that bullet has your fucking name on it. Don't waste it on me. No reason for us to both suffer. Do what needs to be done. Die on your own accord."

"What?" she asked, confused on the sheriff's exact intention.

"Load the weapon and think about how you want to die. Ending yourself is better than rotting in this dungeon. The only question you have ever had in your entire life is if your little brothers were alive. Now you know, and look what they've done to you. You have nothing left to live for. There will be no pain, and you will be with your mother. Do what is right. Goodbye, Annette."

With the pain of talking, let alone the moving of his body, the man who had hired her all those years ago had remained calm and spoke clearly and with confidence. He had presented to her the opportunity to not have to endure any suffering. She could not believe the words coming out of his mouth, but more importantly, she could not believe how she did not necessarily think he was wrong.

Holding the pistol in her hand, she released the magazine. As it slid out from the interior of the weapon's grip, her shaky hands, overcome with the emotion of the moment, missed it, and it hit the ground. Picking up the magazine, she pressed the single round into the top and felt the pressure of the internal spring push back against her thumb as if it was trying to make her change her mind.

Placing the magazine back into the grip, she centered the bottom on her left palm and forced it up and into place. Walking over to the sheriff, she looked back at the door one more time, hoping for some reason or another one of her brothers would open it. The door remained shut as Henderson stepped over the sheriff's slumped body, slipping just a little bit on his expelled blood. Bending over to the counter, she blew out the candle, leaving the two of them in complete darkness.

Holding the pistol in her right hand, she shuffled back to a spot on the floor that she felt was directly across from the sheriff. With her left hand placed on top of the slide, she pulled back, racking the only round she had out of the magazine and into the firing chamber.

Pulling the hammer back and into place, the metal clicking sound seemed to echo throughout the pitch-black cabin. Gripping the weapon firmly, her finger moved its way down to the trigger, which felt colder than the rest of the exposed metal on the body of the gun.

As her eyes adjusted to the darkness, it was still not enough to see anything more than the frail outline of her boss next to her. He had been silent since saying goodbye, and she was unsure if he was dead or not. At this point, it no longer mattered. Feeling the cold metal of the trigger against her skin, she closed her eyes, which now were filled with tears, and said,

"Be the snake, not the mouse."

23 Muricide

From the river bank where the twins stood still making small talk in an attempt to avoid discussing what exactly they had just done, the sound as the pistol sent the round from its barrel was nothing more than a muffled pop. Had they not been intently waiting to hear it; it could have easily gone completely unnoticed. With firsthand knowledge of how loud the sound of a gun firing was inside the small room, Tomek was surprised at what little he heard from their current position.

"There, she did it. Let's go get her. She has proven herself enough," Tomek said.

"Did what, Tomek? Did what?" Drake said.

"She killed him. You know she did. Let's go get her out of there."

"Maybe she is the one who died. Have you thought about that?"

Tomek looked at his brother, then back at the boulder covering their home. Turning to walk up the rock path, he motioned for Drake to join him.

"She is not Uncle, Drake," Tomek said.

His tone was both tense and comforting. Drake immediately felt like he always had growing up. No one knew him like his twin brother did. Their connection was always so strong that often they felt the same, regardless of the situation. This time was no different. Drake did not want to see another family member dead from a self-inflicted wound, but he knew that locking her in the cabin was the only way to truly flush out her allegiance.

Standing outside the door with his hands on the large rock, he pondered if she had killed the man chained to the wall or not.

"Was she aware this was all just a test, or would she feel as if they had left her to die? Would she take his life out of spite or mercy? Would she take her own out of cowardice? Was she a snake or a mouse?"

With Drake's chest, head, and rib injuries, trying to push the rock from its settled-in spot on top of the door would be a futile waste of energy. Electing to sit on the side hill with this back against the slope, Drake placed both of his feet high on the boulder. Tomek joined in placing his legs against the same slope, which provided a back rest for his brother. Both boys pushed as they extended their strong legs, and the top-heavy rock swayed back and forth, rocking it with a push as if it was one of their sleds loaded with firewood and stuck in the snow.

Utilizing the momentum they had built up, the rock tipped over its rolling point and rolled down the hill, gaining speed as it proceeded until reaching its final resting place, splashing down into the river's flowing water with a thunderous entrance. Finding amusement in watching the rolling rock, they again were both thinking on the same wavelength.

"That would make a great ..." Drake started.

"... Trap," Drake and Tomek said in unison.

Smirking at the amusement they both found in the moment, they looked below them at the crushed oak tree door.

"Hope it didn't hurt the hinges. That would not be good," Drake said.

Tomek looked over the construction of the door's framing and was happy to see nothing drastically damaged. "Nope, I think we are fine."

Twisting the handle and pulling the door open, the smell of fresh ignited gun powder filled the air. There was also a dampness that neither of them recalled being present just moments before when they last were in their home. The only light coming into the room was from the open door. Both of them shuffled their feet across the darkness of the room, not wanting to trip over any one of the multiple items that were strewn about.

"Annette," Drake said. "Annette, are you here?"

There was no answer, but there was a peculiar sound coming from the furnace room, which was dug back into the hillside. A dull roaring that neither of them could account for filled the air. The moisture in the air was more and more noticeable with each passing minute.

"What is that?" Tomek asked while remaining in the shadows provided by the door light.

"Stay here. I'll go look," Drake said.

"Check both of their bodies on the way down there," Tomek urged.

"That's my plan. Guard the door. If anyone but me comes up from that tunnel, kill them. "

"Check the bodies!" Tomek demanded.

"I did," Drake replied.

"And …?"

"There is only one here," Drake said, making his way down the dark tunnel with no light.

Moving only by feel with his back against one side of the wall in a shadow fashion, to minimize the square footage of his body exposed to an attack, Drake held tactical knifes in both hands with the one in his left pointed blade down, ready for a strike.

"Which one is missing?" Tomek asked.

Hearing his brother's response from down the tunnel was nearly impossible over the dull roar that was growing in volume by the minute. Unable to stand and not knowing which body his twin had found, Tomek's lack of patience overtook his duty to protect the door.

Sliding his feet across the floor, he felt the wetness of the blood that had poured out of each wound during the battle he had with the sheriff. Reaching the spot on the wall where he felt the chain still connected to the bear trap, he worked his hands down. Feeling the cold metal of the trap's jagged teeth, Tomek was relieved to feel the flesh of his enemy's body. The sheriff lay there, motionless, breathless, lumped, cold, and dead.

"*Where is she?*" Tomek thought to himself. He attempted to look down the tunnel, but the darkness provided no clue as he could see no more than a few feet ahead of himself.

"Drake, you find her?" Tomek yelled out again, hearing a reply from his brother but unable to make out exactly what was being said.

Drake returned to the door, and in an attempt to pry it all the way open to let in as much light as possible, he felt the entire wood shift and drop a few inches into place. Looking over what he could not see from the outside, it was clear that the heavy oak that had kept them safe, warm, and hidden for so many years was broken from their use of the boulder. It was able to open and close, but pushing it over enough for it to remain propped open was no longer an option. Holding onto the door in order to keep it from closing completely, out of both fear of it not opening and the need for some type of light, Tomek braced the wood on the roundness of his shoulder blade. While bearing the weight, he reached around in the dark feeling for something he could place in the jamb in order to keep it slightly propped.

Drake yelled again from the tunnel area of the furnace room, and Tomek had no clue what he was saying. Only able to make out the word "help," Tomek's fingers reached across something smooth, curved, and hard on the floor. Tomek picked it up and immediately realized he held the rib bone from one of the original twin hunters that he had kept as a trophy. Jamming the rib between the wood frame on the interior of the door and the outside ground allowed him to leave the door propped open about six inches.

Leaving the door, he raced back toward the sheriff's body and entered the tunnel. After only taking three bounds in the dark, he slammed into the wall, losing his balance, and falling to the hard dirt floor. Only when he landed, it was not hard, compacted earth that he felt. The coldness of the water he had splashed down into was ten inches deep.

Getting back up to his feet, he yelled for his brother.

"Drake, where are you?"

Finally, close enough to hear the response, he rushed through the knee-deep water upon hearing Drake yell, "Furnace room is flooding! Get down here!"

Turning the corner into the furnace room, the water was considerably deeper. Unable to see in the pitch black, the coldness of the water rushing in at the depth of his chest took his breath away.

"Where is it coming from?" Tomek yelled.

"That fucking boulder must have taken out the smoke valve and created some form of suction! I'm holding this log up trying to block it. Help me grab onto that end!" his brother responded, trying to shake the rising water out of the way of his mouth.

"We are not going to be able to stop it. Let's go!" Tomek yelled, standing next to his brother over the rushing water pouring in through the eight-inch chimney pipe.

"Run!" Drake said as he released the log.

The overpowering blast of river water rushing into the small furnace room was like being hit with a tidal wave. Drake's plug was not stopping the flood, but it was building up pressure in the tube. That pressure knocked both of them down into the deeper water, causing them to flip and turn under the tow with no control.

Once hitting the ground and walls, they regained their orientation and pushed off the bottom with their feet lifting their heads above the water line. With only a foot between the quickly rising water and the ceiling of the furnace room, Tomek heard his brother's voice in the dark.

"This way! The door is here. We have to swim back out of the tunnel and get out!"

"Let's go, then!" Tomek replied with a half-gargled voice, due to the water in his mouth.

Pressing their heads above the water, turning them sideways and putting their ears against the ceiling in order to take what would either be their last breath or the one that would save their lives, the twins filled their lungs with as much air as they could hold. Diving underwater, pushing off of the ceiling with their hands, they both knew that after leaving the furnace room, a left turn would take them back up the tunnel to the main living quarters.

The sloped design of the tunnel itself provided them with the advantage of the lower areas filling with the river water first. Running short on breath, Drake's head crested the water. Grabbing onto Drake's leg, Tomek pulled himself up to meet him above the water line as they both gasped for air, blowing water out of their lungs and mouth.

"We made it," Tomek said, relived.

"We made it through the tunnel, at least. Let's get out of here. Go to the door," Drake said.

"What about her?" Tomek asked.

Walking quickly, still through the dark, the twins made their way up the dry tunnel toward the brightness of the light being let in by the door. With the water still rushing in behind them, the tunnel would be full in less than a minute, and the room would not take long after that.

"She has to be in here somewhere. We have to get her out!" Tomek said, this time grabbing on to his brother's arm to make sure he was listening.

"Dead or alive, I don't know what she is or who she is. Come on, man. Forget her. She's not the same as us. She is not a twin. She was never part of our life, never part of our plan. She is not a child of Uncle and never will be. We would have had to kill her, anyway. She is nothing but a mouse," Drake said while turning the corner into the living room, stepping over the body of the sheriff.

The light extruding from the half-opened door was a welcomed sight. The fact that Henderson was standing in the doorway having heard everything Drake just said was not. The twins stopped where they stood, looking at their sister while wiping the water from their faces that ran down from their soaked hair. The light behind her framed her as if she was some sort of an angel sent to save them. Only she was not an angel. Henderson was a survivor, a fighter, and she stood there between the boys and freedom. Climbing out of the door, she looked at them in disbelief after having heard her own brother's thoughts regarding her life.

"You were both right," she said. "That boulder did make a good trap. Only I was the bait, and here you are looking death in the eye. I may be a mouse, but this mouse always has an escape plan. And one more thing, Drake. You might be a snake, but snakes can't breathe underwater."

With that, she kicked out the rib, slamming the door shut. The dead tree that had been the first line of defense their entire lives was now the top of their coffin, locking them into the rapidly filling pit of water.

24 Fratricide

Again in the dark, the brothers bumped into one another as they raced to the door using only their sense of touch to locate the handle. Turning it and pushing up as they normally would produced no results. The bitter cold of the river water began to remove the dexterity in their hands. Tomek could feel the inner workings of the lock system freely spinning as if they were not engaged at all; as if the entire door was broken. Drake pushed him aside, only to have the same results.

"Push on it! Push with me!" Drake yelled, placing his shoulder into the door. Tomek joined him in the fruitless attempt at budging the heavy slab of oak. Looking behind them, the water continued to rise as it had now engulfed the entire tunnel and was starting to pour into the living quarters where they stood.

"How do we get out?" Tomek asked in a calm voice. The gravity of the situation had not yet hit him as hard as it had his brother. Tomek had figured Drake had a plan all along. This made hearing his twin brother's response all the more painful.

"We don't," said Drake.

And with that they continued slamming their shoulders and backs into the door as hard as they could, feeling it beginning to budge with each impact.

"Come on. We've got to break this damn thing off its frame," Drake said, with the water level already up to his knees and rising every second.

With each slam, Henderson could see the door shift from the outside. She watched each one, knowing that the brothers she had strived so long to save would soon be dead because of her. As horrible as she knew she would feel in the future, at this moment there was no room for empathy or grace. Had she not kicked out the trophy rib, she would have met a worse fate than drowning at the hands of the boys.

The slams grew closer and closer together, and the tree door raised up and fell back down a little more with each one. She could tell the water was getting higher as each impact was less severe due to them not being able to run at the door. The slams were coming at a rapid pace, but there was no yelling. No screaming, no pleading, no begging, no arguing. Just impacts.

Henderson threw her body weight down onto the rounded tree door in an attempt to provide just a little more bracing. She could feel all four of their hands against the door, pushing up with each attempt at reaching breathable air. Again and again she lay there, feeling her brothers trying to fight death. With her head flat against the bark, she could hear the room filling with water. She could hear the splashes of them moving around which preceded each impact.

Just as fast as the impacts were coming, lifting herself and the door partially up, they were gone. No more splashing, no more slamming. Just the sound of running water coming from inside the cabin. With her hands draped down around the sides of the tree, she felt the cold river water as it escaped from the cracks in the frame. With the top of the door being at the ceiling of the cabin, she knew the entire room was flooded, and it was over.

The mouse had survived.

Henderson got back up to her feet and walked toward the river through the switch grass, ignoring the rock patch Drake had taught her to use just hours earlier. Reaching the river, she could not help but look at the boulder lying there in the cold rushing water. The top third of the rock stood out of the water, causing a small set of swirling white foamy rapids around it. Henderson looked, tried to think of some type of metaphor for how the rock had saved her, but she was unable to be clever in the moment. A simple shoulder shrug was all she could offer as she knew that the boulder there in the water was the reason she was alive.

Stumbling down the river bank, she knew she was miles from Pine Run. She knew that no one would believe her story until she showed them the truth. She knew she was now the only cop in town. Not only had the murders of the Senator's baseball-playing hunter sons been solved, so had the homicide of three lawmen and a K-9. She knew she would have to answer the questions, and she knew many would blame her. For so long in her life she was the one with the questions. Now she had the answers, and she would never again have to wonder if her brothers were alive or not.

Crawling into the dugout canoe she and Drake had beached, all these thoughts ran through her mind. For now, though, none of them mattered. Placing her hands against the algae-covered rocks and pushing off, the canoe was taken over by the current. Henderson laid down in the boat and closed her eyes, just the way Drake had originally found her. This time, the canoe effortlessly slid its way past the bend. Had it done so the first time, her entire world would have been much different.

Deputy Annette Henderson was headed downstream floating toward Pine Run and never looked back. For had she taken one last glance behind her, she would certainly have had one more unanswered question.

"How?"

The End ~ Book 1

What did Henderson not see?

What happens when she returns to Pine Run?

Find out in Twins of Prey II ~ Homecoming.

To purchase book two visit the link to my website below:

https://wchoffman.weebly.com/twins-of-prey.html

Join My "New Release" Mailing List

Want to stay up to date with W.C. Hoffman? All members receive a FREE SHORT STORY and discounted prices on future books.

https://wchoffman.weebly.com

SPECIAL THANKS

To my parents: Thank you for pushing me to not just reach for the stars, but to grab one.

To my sisters: Angela Common & Kayce Hathaway. You girls are amazing sisters and even better aunts.

To my editorial team: John McKay, Ken Magee, Daphne Porat, Josh Hawkins and Sara Mack.

To my beta readers: Jessica Ravizza, Eric Steinhoff, Matthew Workman, Kayce Hathaway and Daphne Porat.

To Dr. Bruce Rubenstein: The best story teller I know and the single reason I attended any classes on a daily basis.

To my Military Adviser: Staff Sergeant Jose E. Flores II United States Marine Corps.

To my KickStarter Backers: Greg & Linda Hathaway, Dennis & Kara Maser, Ken Magee, Anthony & Jessica Ravizza, Logan Engels, Christopher Chan, Kayce Hathaway, Dustin & Rachel Scharrer, Justin Ketchum, Nick Tomczak, Joshua Frost and Andrew Bullen.

To the retailers who believe in local authors:
Fenton's Open Book, Sunry's Archery, Jay's Sporting Goods, Bridge Street Exchange, Spot Shooter Archery, and Landgea.

To my friends in the outdoors Industry:
Michigan Bowhunters, Land-O-Lakes Bowmen, From the Blind, Up North Journal, Shawn & Kathy Team Jinx, Michigan Deer Track'n Hounds, Times Up Outdoors, Mike Avery Outdoors,
Dave Cochran Owner/Manager of Show me the Bucks,

Made in the USA
Columbia, SC
22 February 2023

12833472R00114